A READER'S GUIDE

TO THE WORKS OF

HAKIM IBN ADAM

CENTRE FOR STUDIES IN MATTER, MIND, AND MEANING

THREE ROSES PUBLISHING

DEDICATION

*To those who refuse to separate
matter, mind, and meaning.*

THE WORKS

The works of Hakim Ibn Adam are published through Three Roses Publishing (threerosespublishing.com).

The Monographs

Finding Meaning Between Matter and Mind
ISBN: 978-1-9990656-8-3
The most accessible monograph. Begins with the puzzle of consciousness in a physical world, surveys inadequate responses (materialism, idealism, dualism), and builds the participatory alternative step by step. Emphasizes lived implications and invites readers to test the framework against their own experience. Serves as an entry point to the larger Project.

Recommended for: New readers or those seeking a concise introduction to the philosophical framework.

An Inquiry into First Principles: Towards Conscious Participation in an Unfolding Reality
ISBN: 978-1-9990656-6-9
The foundational theoretical work that systematically examines first principles across science, philosophy, and contemplative traditions. Integrates process philosophy (Whitehead), relational ontology (contemporary physics),

and participatory epistemology (Sufi and other traditions) into a comprehensive framework. The longest and most technically demanding of the monographs.

Recommended for: Readers with a philosophical background seeking the full theoretical architecture.

Knowledge Coordination Patterns: Twelve Historical Experiments in Interdisciplinary Coordination.

ISBN: 978-1-9990656-7-6

Surveys twelve historical figures who attempted to integrate multiple domains of knowledge: Pythagoras, Plato, Avicenna, al-Bīrūnī, Aquinas, Leonardo, Leibniz, Goethe, Teilhard de Chardin, Muhammad Iqbal, Carl Jung, and David Bohm. Extracts four heuristic principles while maintaining critical distance from all figures examined. Develops the concept of "coordination without unification."

Recommended for: Readers interested in the history of ideas, or seeking methodological guidance for interdisciplinary work.

Naught Is Like Unto Him: Divine Transcendence in Islamic Thought

ISBN: 978-1-9990656-5-2

Examines the Islamic theological tradition's treatment of divine transcendence (tanzīh) and immanence (tashbīh), focusing on the Ashʿarite school, al-Ghazali's occasionalism, and Ibn Arabi's doctrine of tajallī (theophanic self-disclosure). Shows how classical Islamic thought navigated the tension between God's utter otherness and intimate presence. Connects these theological resources to contemporary consciousness studies.

Recommended for: Readers interested in Islamic philosophy and theology, or seeking the theological dimensions of participatory process monism.

Participatory Process Monism: A Philosophical Framework.

ISBN: 978-1-0698983-3-3

The systematic statement of the framework that underlies the entire Project. Develops a comprehensive metaphysics integrating four Islamic philosophical traditions—Ash'arite occasionalism, Ṣadrian process metaphysics, Akbarian theophanic ontology, and Dāmādian temporal analysis—with contemporary consciousness studies and physics. Addresses the hard problem through panexperientialism, the measurement problem through participatory actualization, and the combination problem through existential intensification. Includes detailed differentiation from Whiteheadian process philosophy, showing how theophanic monism diverges from Process Theology. Concludes with engagement with objections—theological, philosophical, scientific, and methodological—and acknowledged limitations.

Recommended for: Readers seeking the definitive articulation of the philosophical framework, or those interested in the integration of Islamic metaphysics with contemporary philosophy of mind.

The Fiction

The Ancient Bargain

ISBN: 978-1-0698983-2-6

A philosophical closet drama staged in the cytoplasm of a single cell. Two voices—Ribosome and Mitochondrion—debate identity, inheritance, and meaning against the backdrop of the cell's decision whether to live or die. Bracketed stage directions provide physiological fact; the dialogue extracts philosophical meaning. Explores the maternal thread of mitochondrial inheritance, the wound of endosymbiotic capture, and the light (biophotons) that metabolism emits. The most formally innovative work in the Project.

Recommended for: Readers with a background in cell biology, or those seeking the molecular scale of philosophical inquiry.

What Is It Like to Be?
ISBN: 978-1-0698983-0-2
A dialogue between a human philosopher-scientist and an artificial intelligence, conducted over predawn encounters. Each encounter is marked by a different coffee preparation method (French press, pour-over, Moka pot, and ibrīq). Probes the question of machine consciousness through Western theories (Integrated Information Theory) and Islamic philosophy (occasionalism, the divine names). Concludes that relation precedes verification—that we must attend and care before we can know.

Recommended for: Readers interested in AI consciousness, or seeking the ethical implications of uncertain interiority.

Four Meditations on Consciousness and Exile
ISBN: 978-1-0698983-1-9
A collection of four novellas, also published separately, tracing a single protagonist through different thresholds of understanding:

The Divided Light.
ISBN: 978-1-9990656-3-8
A cell biologist encounters consciousness in matter; traces his journey through Western philosophy to mystical recognition. Dense, participatory prose.

Not About Nothing.
ISBN: 978-1-9990656-9-0
Eight fragmentary sections examining exile—geographical,

methodological, existential. The most personally revealing work. Asks whether the exchange was worth it.

The Sea Does Not Care.
ISBN: 978-1-9990656-4-5
A single day in Alexandria, structured by the sun's movement. Long flowing sentences enact process philosophy through prose. The sea's indifference locates meaning precisely.

The Sun That Remembers.
ISBN: 978-1-9990656-2-1
Visions traverse human history from cave painters to contemporary consciousness studies. At sunset, seeking ends; recognition arrives. The culmination of the four meditations.

Recommended for: Readers who prefer narrative to argument, or who seek the experiential dimension of philosophical insight.

CONTENTS

INTRODUCTION

The Name as Philosophical Act

The name "Hakim Ibn Adam" is a philosophical statement. It enacts the work's central thesis: that the individual self is not the ultimate locus of knowing. By setting aside the biographical details that might invite psychological interpretation, the name clears the space for universality. The questions addressed here are not about one person's journey; they are questions about consciousness and reality that any human being might ask.

The name itself carries the argument. In Arabic, *ḥakīm* means both "sage" and "physician"—a conjunction that invokes an older unity of knowledge where healing the body and contemplating reality were aspects of a single inquiry. *Ibn Adam* means "son of Adam," or everyman—a bearer of the breath breathed into the first human form. Together, the name refuses the particularity of autobiography while insisting on the universality of the human condition. Whoever speaks through these works does so as a representative instance of consciousness struggling to understand itself.

Yet the name also honors a specific "personal geography": from the Near East to the West, from cell biology to mystical inquiry. This is not "Anonymous" or "A

Seeker," but a name with linguistic roots and traditional weight. It signals that the author speaks from within a heritage, utilizing Islamic philosophical vocabulary not as ornament but as instrument—providing concepts that Western philosophy lacks and distinctions that the scientific worldview cannot generate.

Hakim Ibn Adam is not hiding; he is choosing what to show. Withheld are the credentials that would authorize or disqualify claims in advance. Shown is a mind formed by scientific training and mystical inheritance, working at the intersection of disciplines that rarely speak to each other. The name permits the work to be read as what it is: an extended meditation on consciousness, exile, and participation, offered by someone who has spent a lifetime preparing to offer it.

The Life Glimpsed Through the Fiction

The author declines to provide conventional biographical information, but the fiction is not silent about the life that generated it. Across the novellas, a figure emerges—not identical from work to work, but recognizably continuous, a single consciousness encountered at different thresholds.

For more than thirty years, he studied how cells decide to live or die. The technical vocabulary of the fiction is not decorative; it emerges from intimate acquaintance with confocal microscopes and apoptosis assays, with calcium transients and stress granules, with the molecular machinery that maintains life at the cellular level. When *The Divided Light* describes a T-lymphocyte refusing its programmed death, the description carries the weight of actual observation. The author has watched thousands of cells die through a microscope. He knows what it looks like when one hesitates.

He is an exile. The recurring figure in the novellas left home—somewhere in the Near East, the fiction implies without specifying—with one suitcase. He went West to acquire knowledge that could not be acquired at home. He succeeded. But the cost of this success was permanent displacement. "The self is not portable," one novella observes. "You cannot pack it in a suitcase, carry it across oceans, set it down unchanged."

This exile is both geographical and epistemological. The young scientist who embraced molecular biology found in it a world that made sense—sequences and structures, mechanisms and pathways, questions that had answers. Unlike the social world, which kept demanding that he explain his origins and translate his heritage, the laboratory judged him only by his data. This was freedom, or so it seemed. But the price of entry was reduction: the self simplified to fit through doorways built for different shapes, the tradition flattened into something that could be explained in a sentence. "He became fluent in two kinds of reduction," one novella notes, "the cultural and the methodological. Both promised the same thing—acceptance purchased through simplification."

He carries a mystical inheritance. The grandfather appears in several works—a poet, a contemplator of divine names, a man who would have looked at a nematode and seen not a mechanism but a miracle. This grandfather never published in peer-reviewed journals and never built a career in a world that had no place for him. His mode of knowing was dismissed as unscientific, his questions as unanswerable. The grandson, trained in the laboratory's precision, cannot simply return to the grandfather's vision. But neither can he forget it. The questions that seemed answered by molecular biology keep reopening. The mechanism cannot explain the meaning. The cell that hesitates appears to be doing something more than chemistry.

And so the scientist becomes a philosopher—"by necessity," as the author puts it. The questions accumulated until they demanded a different form of investigation.

The Institutional Frame

An Independent Publisher, Three Roses Publishing, publishes the books, but the scholarly works bear an additional affiliation: the Centre for Studies in Matter, Mind, and Meaning. The Centre's stated mission is "to produce scholarly work that integrates scientific inquiry, philosophical analysis, and spiritual reflection."

This institutional frame, modest as it appears, announces an ambition that the contemporary academy broadly prohibits. The modern research university is organized around specialization. Philosophers do not conduct laboratory experiments; biologists do not publish on Islamic metaphysics; scholars of religion do not engage with quantum mechanics. Each discipline guards its methods, its standards, and its territory. The result is what the monographs call 'knowledge fragmentation'—sophisticated understanding within domains, incoherence between them.

The Centre for Studies in Matter, Mind, and Meaning positions itself against this fragmentation. Its very name insists that these three terms—matter, mind, and meaning—belong together, that a complete understanding of any one requires engagement with the others. Matter without mind becomes a "dull affair", as described by Whitehead. Mind without matter becomes untethered speculation, vulnerable to solipsism and self-deception. Meaning without both becomes mere assertion, lacking the grounding that only rigorous inquiry can provide.

The Centre is not a building or an endowment. It is better understood as a declaration of intellectual intent—a statement that certain questions matter, that certain integrations are necessary, that the work of synthesis must continue even when the institutions of knowledge make little room for it.

The Dedications

A writer's dedications reveal what they consider themselves

to be doing. The dedications in Hakim Ibn Adam's works form their own quiet commentary on the Project.

An Inquiry into First Principles is dedicated "to the obstacles and failures that opened the door to this inquiry." This is not false modesty. The author acknowledges that the work emerges from crisis—from the breakdown of frameworks that once seemed adequate, from questions that could not be answered within the disciplines that posed them. The obstacles were not detours from the path; they were the path.

Four Meditations on Consciousness and Exile bears a dedication that cuts deeper: "And to those who taught us, loved us, and let us go." The "letting go" is ambiguous and therefore resonant. Parents let children go when they leave for distant universities; teachers let students go when they have learned what can be taught; traditions let their inheritors go when the old forms no longer suffice. The dedication honours these releases while acknowledging their cost.

The Ancient Bargain is dedicated "To the Unbroken Chain," followed by a passage after Ibn Arabi: "The cosmos is the Breath of the Merciful—each creature a word exhaled by the Real, suspended in being for a moment, then released." Here, the dedication opens onto the theological vision that underlies the entire Project. The "unbroken chain" is the lineage of transmission, the continuity that connects each generation to what came before. But it is also the molecular continuity that the novella explores—the mitochondrial DNA passed only through mothers, the ribosomal RNA that has been folding proteins since before DNA learned to archive, the gradient that has not stopped flowing for more than two billion years.

Finding Meaning Between Matter and Mind takes the widest address: "To all seekers who dare to wonder what reality is, and who never stop asking how they fit within it." This dedication positions the reader not as a consumer of a product but as a fellow inquirer into questions that cannot be definitively answered. The book is offered to those who share the author's restlessness, his refusal to accept the available answers, and his insistence that the question of meaning cannot be dissolved by either scientific reduction or religious dogma.

PART I

THE PROJECT

CHAPTER 1

THE CENTRAL PROBLEM

What does it mean to be conscious in a world that appears to need no consciousness to function?

This question, posed in the introduction to *Four Meditations on Consciousness and Exile*, is the engine that drives everything Hakim Ibn Adam has written. The question takes other forms: How does awareness arise from matter that has none? What is the relationship between the felt quality of experience and the physical processes that seem to produce it? Why is there something it is like to be you, rather than nothing? These are not different questions but different facets of the same question.

It is not a puzzle that admits of a clever solution, to be answered and set aside. It is a wound—a fracture at the foundation of modern thought that makes our most sophisticated understanding of reality paradoxically uninhabitable for the conscious beings who produced it.

This chapter examines that wound: how it opened, what symptoms it produces, and why the obvious remedies fail.

THE SPLIT

Somewhere in the seventeenth century, Western thought made a fateful decision. It divided the world into two kinds of stuff.

On one side: matter. Extended, measurable, subject to mathematical laws. The world of physics—particles in motion, forces acting at distances, quantities that could be precisely determined. This was the world that science would study, and study with unprecedented success. Galileo, Newton, and their successors built a picture of the physical universe so powerful that it seemed to leave nothing unexplained.

On the other side: mind. Thinking, feeling, experiencing. The inner world of consciousness that each of us knows directly—the redness of red, the ache of grief, the taste of coffee. This was the world that seemed to resist measurement, that could not be weighed or located in space, that belonged to the subject rather than the object.

René Descartes gave this division its classic formulation: *res extensa* (extended substance) and *res cogitans* (thinking substance). Matter takes up space; mind thinks. They are fundamentally different kinds of things.

This split was not merely a philosophical abstraction. It shaped the entire development of modern science and, through science, the modern world. To study nature scientifically meant to bracket consciousness, to describe the world as it would be without any observer, to achieve what the philosopher Thomas Nagel called "the view from nowhere." The scientist must erase herself from her observations to achieve objectivity. Personal experience, feeling, meaning—these were not data but noise, to be eliminated from serious inquiry.

The strategy worked. Physics progressed from Newton to Einstein to quantum mechanics, achieving predictive precision that would have seemed miraculous to earlier ages. Chemistry explained the composition of matter. Biology revealed the mechanisms of life. The material world yielded its secrets to investigators who systematically ignored their own consciousness to study everything else.

But success came at a cost. The more completely science described the physical world, the less room there seemed to be for the mind that was doing the describing. Consciousness became an embarrassment—real beyond doubt (for what could be more certain than that you are having experiences right now?), yet impossible to locate within the scientific picture. As the philosopher Alfred North Whitehead diagnosed it, nature had been "bifurcated"—split against itself. The qualities that make life worth living—colour, beauty, meaning, purpose—were exiled from the "real" world of colourless particles in motion and relocated to a mental realm whose very existence became increasingly difficult to explain.

THREE SYMPTOMS OF THE CRISIS

The wound at the heart of modern thought manifests in at least three persistent problems that have resisted solution for centuries. These are not minor technical difficulties awaiting the next breakthrough in research. They are structural failures that reveal something wrong in our basic assumptions.

The Hard Problem of Consciousness

The first symptom is what the philosopher David Chalmers named "the hard problem." The problem is this: even if we describe in complete physical detail every process in your brain when you see the colour red—every neuron firing, every chemical released, every electrical pattern—we seem to have left out the most important thing. We have not explained why seeing red *feels* like anything at all. Why is there something it-is-like-to-be you, rather than nothing?

The physical story, however complete, describes structure and function. It tells us which neurons connect to which, how information flows through the system, and what outputs result from which inputs. But experience is not structure or function. Experience is *what-it-is-like*—the qualitative feel of pain or pleasure, the specific character of seeing blue versus seeing green, the taste of chocolate that no amount of chemical description captures.

You could know everything about the physics and chemistry of chocolate—every molecule, every receptor, every neural pathway—without ever having tasted chocolate yourself. And if you then tasted it for the first time, you would learn something new: what chocolate tastes like. This *"something new"* is not information about structure or function. It is the experience itself.

Finding Meaning Between Matter and Mind poses the problem starkly: "You can't get something from nothing. If you start with ingredients that have zero experience, zero consciousness, zero inner life—and you just arrange them in different patterns—when does experience suddenly appear? At what level of complexity does the light turn on? And why?"

The usual response is to invoke "emergence"—consciousness emerges from complex physical organization, the way liquidity emerges from water molecules. But this analogy fails precisely where it matters most. Liquidity is just a description of how molecules behave collectively; there is no mystery about how molecular motion produces wetness. Consciousness is not like that. It is not merely a description of how neurons behave. It is the felt reality of experience itself—and you cannot derive experience from ingredients that have no capacity for feeling, no matter how cleverly you arrange them.

Some philosophers, recognizing this impasse, have concluded that consciousness must be an illusion—that there is nothing it-is-like-to-be you, that the feeling of experience is itself a kind of trick played by neural processes. But as Galen Strawson observed, this is the strangest thing that has ever happened in the whole history of human thought. To deny consciousness is to deny the very medium through which the denial is formulated and understood. The one thing we cannot coherently doubt is that we are having experiences.

The Measurement Problem in Physics

The second symptom emerges from physics itself—the very discipline that was supposed to describe reality without reference to consciousness.

Quantum mechanics is our most successful physical theory, capable of predictions verified to extraordinary precision. Yet at its heart lies a puzzle that has resisted resolution for a century: the measurement problem.

According to quantum mechanics, a particle does not have a definite position or momentum until it is measured. Before measurement, it exists in a "superposition"—a blur of possibilities described by a mathematical wave function. The wave function evolves smoothly and deterministically according to the Schrödinger equation. But the moment a measurement occurs, something discontinuous happens: the wave function "collapses" to a definite state, and the particle is found in one specific location.

What counts as a measurement? When exactly does the collapse occur? The theory cannot say. The mathematical formalism describes what happens before measurement and what results after, but the transition itself—the moment when possibility becomes actuality—remains unexplained within the theory.

This would be merely a technical puzzle if it did not point to something more profound. The measurement problem suggests that observation plays a fundamental role in physics that physics cannot itself account for. The observer, supposedly eliminated from the scientific picture, returns to the foundations of the most basic science.

Some interpretations try to avoid this conclusion. The

"many-worlds" interpretation proposes that all possible outcomes occur, each in a separate branch of an ever-dividing multiverse, eliminating collapse by eliminating the uniqueness of measurement. But this interpretation cannot explain why we experience only one branch rather than the superposition of all branches. The observer problem is not solved; it is merely displaced.

Other interpretations, like QBism (Quantum Bayesianism), take the opposite approach, treating quantum states as subjective degrees of belief rather than objective states of reality. This elegantly dissolves certain paradoxes, but only by making the observer fundamental to physical theory—precisely what materialist philosophy sought to avoid.

The measurement problem reveals that even our most fundamental physics requires something it cannot explain: an observer, a consciousness, a perspective from which possibilities become actualities. The bifurcation that was supposed to make science possible turns out to undermine it at its foundations.

The Meaning Crisis

The third symptom is not philosophical but existential. When consciousness cannot locate itself within our best theories of reality, when purpose and value are excluded from the scientific worldview, when the qualities that make life worth living are deemed illusory or secondary, the result is not merely intellectual dissatisfaction. It is what the cognitive scientist John Vervaeke has called a "meaning crisis."

The success of scientific materialism in manipulating and predicting the physical world has come at the cost of rendering that world uninhabitable for conscious beings seeking meaning and purpose. We can explain, with increasing precision, *how* things happen. We cannot say *why* they matter—or whether "mattering" is even coherent within the scientific picture.

The Introduction to *Four Meditations* frames this crisis in terms of exile: "To study consciousness scientifically is to stand outside experience, while experience is all we have." The scientific observer must bracket her own consciousness to achieve objectivity, yet consciousness is the only medium through which objectivity can be recognized or valued. We have exiled ourselves from our own descriptions of reality.

This exile is not merely epistemological. It is, as the Introduction notes, "the same exile" as the existential displacement of the person who leaves home for distant knowledge, who masters new methods and languages while losing connection to origins. The intellectual homelessness of the modern scientific worldview and the personal homelessness of the exile "turn out to be the same exile, approached from different directions."

The meaning crisis manifests in rising rates of depression and anxiety, in the persistent sense that something essential has been lost, in the hunger for significance that consumer culture cannot satisfy. These are not failures of individual adjustment. They are symptoms of a worldview that has no place for what matters most.

Why Choosing Sides Doesn't Help

Faced with these problems, there are two obvious responses. Perhaps the materialist picture is correct, and we simply need to accept that consciousness is an illusion or an epiphenomenon—real in some diminished sense but not fundamental to reality. Or perhaps the opposite is true: consciousness is fundamental, and the physical world is somehow derived from or dependent on mind.

Finding Meaning Between Matter and Mind devotes sustained attention to why neither option works.

The materialist option—"pure matter"—generates the problems we have already seen. It cannot explain how consciousness arises from unconscious ingredients. It cannot account for the observer that physics requires. It leaves meaning homeless. To say that consciousness is "really" just neural activity is to change the subject. Neural activity is what consciousness looks like from outside, described in the third person. It is not what consciousness *is*—the felt reality of experience known from within. You cannot make the inside disappear by describing the outside more precisely.

The idealist option—"pure mind"—has its own difficulties. If the physical world is really a construction or projection of consciousness, why is it so stable and consistent? Why does the table remain solid when you are not looking at it? Why does the sun rise whether or not you are awake to experience it? Your imagination is flexible, responsive to your wishes; you can make a pink elephant appear and disappear at will. But the real world resists your wishes. It has a "stubborn independence" that purely mental constructions lack.

Moreover, the idealist view struggles to explain intersubjectivity—the fact that you and I seem to experience the same world. If reality is just my experience, why do you experience it too? And why do our experiences match so precisely? We can collaborate on building things, conducting experiments, and navigating spaces. The world presents itself consistently to different observers. If everything is in the mind, whose mind is it in?

Finally, idealism cannot explain why science works. We can use mathematics to predict how things will behave with extraordinary precision. We can calculate eclipses, design bridges, and collide particles. These predictions work because there are regular patterns in how things behave—patterns we discover rather than create. If everything is mental, where do these patterns come from? Why these laws and not others?

Finding Meaning draws the conclusion: "Neither extreme works. Reducing everything to unconscious matter doesn't work. Reducing everything to consciousness doesn't work either. The problems aren't solved by choosing sides—they're created by setting up sides in the first place."

THE FALSE ASSUMPTION

Both materialism and idealism share a common assumption: reality must be fundamentally made of one kind of stuff—either matter or mind, either objective or subjective. They differ only in which kinds of stuff are basic and which are derivative. But what if this shared assumption is the problem?

The Introduction to *Four Meditations* hints at the alternative: "the distance between knower and known is itself an artifact of a particular way of organizing experience." The split between matter and mind is not a discovery about reality; it is a choice about how to conceptualize reality. And it may be a choice that creates problems with no solutions because the problems themselves are artifacts of the conceptualization.

What if we started differently? What if we refused the choice between matter and mind, not by finding some clever synthesis but by questioning whether these were ever the right categories in the first place?

This is where Hakim Ibn Adam's work becomes constructive rather than merely diagnostic. The monographs develop a framework—Participatory Process Monism—that attempts to reconceive reality in terms that do not generate the insoluble problems. The fiction explores what it would feel like to inhabit such a reconceived reality, to experience the world as process and participation rather than as dead matter confronting an isolated mind.

But before we can understand the solution, we must feel the full weight of the problem. The wound is real. The crisis is not exaggerated. Our best theories of reality have made consciousness inexplicable, observation mysterious, and meaning homeless. Something has gone wrong at the foundations.

The next chapter examines what the Project proposes in place of the broken framework.

CHAPTER 2

THE FRAMEWORK — PARTICIPATORY PROCESS MONISM

The previous chapter diagnosed a crisis. The modern worldview, for all its predictive power, has split reality in a way that makes consciousness inexplicable, observation mysterious, and meaning homeless. The hard problem of consciousness, the measurement problem in quantum mechanics, and the meaning crisis in contemporary life are not separate puzzles but symptoms of a single wound—a wound opened when Descartes divided reality into thinking substance and extended substance, and left them facing each other across an unbridgeable gulf.

What would it look like to think differently?

The Project's fifth monograph, *Participatory Process Monism: A Philosophical Framework*, develops a comprehensive response to this crisis. The framework does not patch the problems with clever solutions; it dissolves them by changing the terms in which they arise. The term "Participatory Process Monism" is dense with meaning:

monism asserts that reality is ultimately one rather than divided into separate substances; *process* emphasizes that this reality is fundamentally dynamic rather than static; *participatory* indicates that consciousness is not a passive observer but an active participant in reality's actualization.

This chapter unpacks those ideas, traces their sources in Islamic philosophical traditions, shows how they address the problems that the Cartesian framework could only generate, and distinguishes this framework from the Western process philosophy with which it shares certain vocabulary.

THREE FOUNDATIONAL PRINCIPLES

The Primacy of Consciousness

The first principle reverses a deeply ingrained assumption. We are accustomed to thinking that the universe is made of unconscious stuff—particles, fields, forces—and that consciousness somehow emerges late in cosmic history, after billions of years of stellar evolution and biological development, as a byproduct of sufficiently complex neural arrangements.

Participatory Process Monism inverts this picture. Consciousness—or more precisely, experience—is not a late addition to reality but a fundamental feature of it. This does not mean that electrons have thoughts or that rocks contemplate their existence. It means that the division between "experiential" and "non-experiential" is not absolute but admits of degrees. The experience of a fundamental physical process is so minimal that calling it experience at all stretches language. But that minimal interiority is not zero.

The argument proceeds through elimination. If we start with ingredients that have absolutely no experience—no interior character whatsoever, nothing it-is-like-to-be them—then no rearrangement can produce experience. You cannot get something from nothing. Complexity does not help: a billion zeros, however artfully arranged, still sum to zero. The alternative is to start with processes that possess some minimal experiential quality, however faint, and trace how complex consciousness develops through integration and intensification rather than emerging from absolute absence.

This view is called panpsychism in Western philosophy, though *Participatory Process Monism* prefers the term *panexperientialism* to avoid misleading connotations of universal mentality. The Islamic tradition provides its own resources through the Quranic affirmation that all things engage in *tasbīḥ*—divine praise—and the Ṣadrian doctrine that existence (*wujūd*) and finding/consciousness (*wijdān*) share the same linguistic root. To exist is to participate, however minimally, in the experiential character that Islamic philosophy identifies with the self-luminosity of being itself.

The philosophical payoff is immediate. The hard problem—how do you get experience from non-experience?—dissolves. We do not have to explain the emergence of consciousness from the unconscious; we have to explain how simple experiential processes develop, integrate, and intensify into the complex consciousness we know directly in ourselves. This is still difficult, but it is the kind of difficulty that admits of progress rather than the categorical impossibility of deriving something from nothing.

The Priority of Process

The second principle challenges another deep assumption: that the world is made of things—objects, substances, particles that exist and then change. We naturally picture reality as composed of static entities that persist through time, undergoing modifications while remaining fundamentally the same stuff.

Participatory Process Monism reverses this. Reality is not made of things that change but of processes—ongoing events, activities, happenings that constitute what appears as persistent substance. What we call "things" are relatively stable patterns within flux, like eddies in a stream. The eddy is real, but its reality is processual: it is a *happening*, not a *thing*.

Consider a flame. Is a flame an object that undergoes changes, or is it an ongoing process of combustion? You cannot point to any particular molecule and say, "That is the flame." The flame is the pattern of activity, the dynamic transformation of fuel into heat and light. Now extend this insight: what if everything is more like the flame than we typically assume? What if electrons and atoms and organisms are all patterns of activity, processes maintaining themselves through continuous happening?

This is not merely philosophical speculation. Modern physics supports it. In quantum field theory, particles are not tiny objects but excitations of underlying fields— vibrational patterns in something fundamentally dynamic. In biology, organisms are not collections of parts but self-maintaining processes of metabolism and reproduction. Even apparently solid objects are, at the atomic level, mostly empty space filled with patterns of electromagnetic activity.

The Islamic philosophical tradition developed sophisticated process metaphysics centuries before Whitehead. Mullā Ṣadrā's doctrine of substantial motion (*al-ḥarakat al-jawhariyya*) argues that substance itself is in constant flux—not merely that accidents change while substance remains, but that the very being of things is dynamic becoming. Existence is not a static property but an act, an ongoing event. The Ashʿarite doctrine of continuous creation (*khalq jadīd* or *tajdīd al-khalq*) holds that God recreates the world at each instant, with apparent persistence being the result of divine habit (*ʿāda*) rather than inherent substantial endurance.

The convergence of these independent traditions—Whiteheadian process philosophy in the West, Ṣadrian and Ash'arite metaphysics in Islam—suggests that process thinking captures something fundamental about reality rather than being an arbitrary philosophical preference.

The Centrality of Participation

The third principle is perhaps the most radical. We are accustomed to thinking of observation as passive—the mind registers what is already there, the way a camera records a scene. The world exists independently; consciousness merely photographs it.

Participatory Process Monism proposes something different: observation is not passive registration but active participation in the determination of reality. The observer is not an external spectator but a participant in the ongoing process of actualization. Reality is not fully determined until it is engaged, and the engagement shapes what becomes actual.

This idea draws on quantum mechanics, where the measurement problem reveals that observation plays a role physics cannot fully explain. Before measurement, a quantum system exists in superposition—a blend of possibilities described by the wave function. Upon measurement, one possibility becomes actual. What causes this transition? The mathematical formalism of quantum mechanics cannot say. Something happens at measurement that the theory cannot fully capture.

The physicist John Archibald Wheeler, reflecting on quantum mechanics, proposed that we live in a "participatory universe." His analysis of delayed-choice experiments—where decisions made now seem to influence what path a photon took in the past—led him to conclude that the observer is inextricably woven into the fabric of physical reality. "No elementary phenomenon is a phenomenon until it is an observed phenomenon."

The Islamic tradition provides parallel resources. Ash'arite occasionalism holds that what appear as causal connections are really divine habits—regularities in God's continuous creative activity that could in principle differ. This is not caprice but consistency: God sustains the world through reliable patterns while remaining the true agent in all events. Ibn 'Arabī's theophanic metaphysics adds that creation is the ongoing self-disclosure (*tajallī*) of divine reality through the "Divine Names"—attributes that require conscious witnesses for their full manifestation. The cosmos is not a machine running independently but a continuous divine communication that requires reception to be complete.

This is what "participatory" means in Participatory Process Monism. Reality is not a collection of objects waiting to be observed. Reality is an ongoing process of actualization in which observation—conscious engagement—plays a constitutive role.

THE ONTOLOGICAL ARCHITECTURES

Participatory Process Monism grounds its philosophical claims in four distinct but complementary Islamic metaphysical traditions. Each provides essential resources; together they yield a framework unavailable from any single source.

Ash'arite Occasionalism and Temporal Atomism

The Ash'arite school of *kalām* (speculative theology), dominant in Sunni Islam for nearly a millennium, developed a radical occasionalism: God alone possesses genuine causal power. What appear as natural causes—fire burning cotton, stones falling, medicines healing—are in reality divine acts occurring on the occasion of apparent causes. Fire does not burn; God creates burning in cotton when fire is present. The regularity of these patterns reflects divine habit (*'ādat Allāh*) rather than inherent natural necessity.

The Ash'arites coupled this with temporal atomism (*zamān fard*): time itself consists of discrete instants with no continuous flow between them. At each instant, God recreates the world; what we experience as persistence is actually a series of momentary creations whose similarity creates the illusion of continuity. The key doctrine is that accidents cannot persist for two successive instants (*al-'araḍ lā yabqā zamānayn*)—every property, every configuration must be continually renewed.

This metaphysics anticipates quantum mechanics in striking ways. The discreteness of quantum energy states, the probabilistic nature of quantum transitions, the role of observation in determining outcomes—all find structural parallels in occasionalist metaphysics. The quantum world, like the Ash'arite cosmos, does not flow continuously but proceeds through discrete events whose regularities are statistical rather than mechanically deterministic.

Ṣadrian Process Metaphysics

Mullā Ṣadrā (d. 1640) revolutionized Islamic philosophy through two interconnected doctrines. The doctrine of substantial motion (*al-ḥarakat al-jawhariyya*) holds that substance itself—not merely its accidents—is in constant flux. Aristotelian philosophy had maintained that change occurs only in accidents while substance remains stable. Ṣadrā argued that the very being of things continuously transforms, that existence is essentially dynamic rather than static.

His second revolutionary doctrine, the primacy of existence (*aṣālat al-wujūd*), holds that existence is the sole genuine reality while essences are mental abstractions. This overturned the Suhrawardian position that essences are fundamental. If existence is primary, and existence is fundamentally active, then reality is fundamentally processual—a continuous becoming rather than a static being.

Ṣadrā's analysis of existence as admitting of degrees of intensity (*tashkīk al-wujūd*) proves crucial for understanding consciousness. Existence intensifies from the minimal being of prime matter through vegetable and animal life to human consciousness and beyond. Consciousness is not a property added to existence but the self-luminosity that existence possesses in varying degrees. Higher levels of existence are more intensely conscious; the gradation is continuous.

Akbarian Theophanic Ontology

Ibn ʿArabī (d. 1240), the "Greatest Master" (*al-Shaykh al-Akbar*), developed an elaborate metaphysics of divine self-disclosure (*tajallī*). The cosmos, in his view, is not a creation set apart from God but the ongoing manifestation of divine attributes—the "Most Beautiful Names" (*al-asmā' al-husnā*)—through a continuous "Breath of the Merciful" (*nafas al-raḥmān*).

Central to this metaphysics is the doctrine of perpetual creation (*al-khalq al-mutajaddid* or *khalq jadīd*): the world is not created once but continuously renewed at every instant. No two moments of creation are identical; novelty is woven into the fabric of reality. The apparent stability of objects reflects divine consistency, not static substance.

Ibn ʿArabī's concept of the "Fixed Entities" (*al-aʿyān al-thābita*)—the immutable archetypes in divine knowledge that determine what each thing can become—provides crucial resources for understanding the relation between possibility and actuality. These are not Platonic forms existing independently but the content of divine knowledge, eternally known by God, awaiting manifestation in cosmic existence.

The human being occupies a unique position in this metaphysics as the "Perfect Human" (*al-insān al-kāmil*)—the comprehensive mirror in which all divine names achieve simultaneous manifestation. Human consciousness is not an accident of evolution but serves a cosmic function: it is the locus where creation becomes aware of itself, where the divine self-disclosure achieves completion through conscious witness.

Dāmādian Temporal Architectures

Mīr Dāmād (d. 1631), teacher of Mullā Ṣadrā, developed perhaps the most sophisticated analysis of time in the history of philosophy. He distinguished multiple temporal modalities: *sarmad* (absolute eternity—the relation of the permanent to the permanent); *dahr* (perpetuity—the relation of the permanent to the changing); *zamān* (serial time—the relation of the changing to the changing); and *waqt* (the lived present—the intersection of all temporal modes in conscious experience).

This multi-tiered temporal architecture proves essential for reconciling the block universe of relativity theory with the experienced flow of time. At the *dahrī* level, all events coexist in atemporal order—what physics calls the four-dimensional manifold. At the *zamānī* level, events occur in succession, with genuine before and after. The transition between these levels—from atemporal order to temporal becoming—occurs through conscious experience, which occupies the *waqt* where different temporal modes intersect.

Mīr Dāmād's concept of "perpetual origination" (*ḥudūth dahrī*) provides a middle path between creation in time and eternal necessity. The cosmos is neither a temporal event that began nor an eternal necessity coexistent with God; it is perpetually originated in the *dahrī* realm, continuously dependent on its divine source while having no temporal beginning. This framework illuminates contemporary cosmological questions about the Big Bang's relation to temporal beginning.

THE EPISTEMOLOGICAL FRAMEWORK

Participatory Process Monism develops a sophisticated epistemology grounded in the Islamic tradition's analysis of knowledge. The framework identifies three complementary modes of knowing, each genuine, each limited, all necessary for comprehensive understanding.

The Triadic Structure

The Quranic categorization of certainty into three ascending levels— *'ilm al-yaqīn* (knowledge of certainty), *'ayn al-yaqīn* (eye of certainty), and *ḥaqq al-yaqīn* (truth of certainty)— provides the foundation.

The first level, knowledge of certainty, corresponds to what the monograph calls the *rational mode*: inferential knowledge gained through demonstration and logical analysis. When one deduces the existence of fire from seeing smoke, or proves a mathematical theorem, one operates at this level. The knowledge is genuine but abstract—one knows *that* something is true without directly experiencing its truth.

The second level, eye of certainty, corresponds to the *empirical mode*: knowledge gained through direct observation and systematic investigation. Moving from inferring fire to witnessing flames transforms knowledge from abstract to concrete. This is the domain of natural science—testing hypotheses against phenomena, refining theories through observation and experiment.

The third level, truth of certainty, corresponds to the *contemplative mode*: knowledge gained through direct recognition that transcends the subject-object structure. This is not merely knowing about fire or seeing fire but being transformed by fire—participatory knowledge in which the knower and known achieve a form of union.

The crucial principle is *non-competition*. These three modes do not fight over the same territory; they reveal complementary aspects of reality. Science maps structural patterns; philosophy reveals logical necessities; contemplative practice discloses qualitative depths. A description of the brain's neural activity is not wrong—it is simply incomplete without the first-person perspective that knows consciousness from within.

Knowledge by Presence

The distinction between knowledge by presence (*'ilm ḥuḍūrī*) and knowledge by representation (*'ilm ḥuṣūlī*), systematically developed by Suhrawardī and refined by later philosophers, proves essential for understanding why consciousness resists objective explanation.

Knowledge by representation operates through mental forms that correspond to external objects. Scientific knowledge is paradigmatically representational: models that map onto phenomena, theories that describe structures. Such knowledge maintains the distinction between knower and known, subject and object.

Knowledge by presence is immediate, non-representational awareness. Self-consciousness exemplifies this mode: when I am aware of myself, this awareness is not mediated by a concept or representation of myself. I do not know myself by forming an internal model; I am directly present to myself. This presence is the self-luminosity that Ṣadrā identifies with the act of existence itself.

The hard problem of consciousness reflects the categorical difference between these modes. No accumulation of representational knowledge can yield knowledge by presence; the qualitative "what it is like" of experience is accessible only from within, through direct acquaintance. This is not a failure of current science but a structural feature of how consciousness relates to knowledge.

DISTINGUISHING PPM FROM WHITEHEADIAN PROCESS PHILOSOPHY

The vocabulary of Participatory Process Monism—"actual occasions," "prehension," "creative advance," "process ontology"—resonates with Alfred North Whitehead's Philosophy of Organism. This terminological kinship invites misreading the framework as "Islamicized Whiteheadianism"—a translation of *Process and Reality*. Such reading would be fundamentally mistaken.

While both frameworks affirm that reality is fundamentally processual, experiential, and relational, they diverge at the deepest metaphysical level. The differences concern not peripheral details but foundational questions: What is ultimate? What is the nature of God? What grounds possibility? What ensures the subject's continuity?

On the Category of the Ultimate

For Whitehead, the ultimate is *Creativity*—a neutral, unconscious principle of novelty that underlies every actual entity, including God. Creativity is not conscious; it is the pure "urge" toward the novel, the principle of "the many becoming one and increased by one." In this scheme, God is not the source of Creativity but its "primordial creature"— the first entity to be instantiated by this neutral metaphysical principle.

This makes Whitehead's system, despite its elegance, structurally atheistic regarding the Absolute. The ultimate is an unconscious force; the conscious Reality (God) is its derivative.

Participatory Process Monism categorically rejects this subordination. Following Mullā Ṣadrā's doctrine of the primacy of existence, the framework holds that God— identified with Pure Existence (*Wujūd Baḥt*)—is the ultimate. There is no Creativity distinct from God because God *is* the infinite activity of Being. What Whitehead attributes to neutral Creativity, PPM understands as divine self-disclosure (*tajallī*) and the Breath of the Merciful (*nafas al-raḥmān*).

This is not a minor theological adjustment. It reorients the entire metaphysical architecture, grounding the dynamism of process in divine will rather than unconscious force.

On the Nature of God

Whitehead constructs a "Dipolar God" with two natures. The *Primordial Nature* is God's conceptual grasp of all possibilities—but Whitehead explicitly states that this nature is "deficient in actuality." The *Consequent Nature* is God's reception of the evolving world—but this means God grows, changes, is affected by worldly events. God needs the world to achieve full actuality.

This "Process Theology" understands divine-world relations as mutual interdependence: God influences the world through persuasive lures; the world contributes to God's ongoing experience. God becomes a "fellow-sufferer who understands" rather than the Absolute who sustains.

Participatory Process Monism offers instead what it calls *Theophanic Monism*. The divine Essence (*Dhāt*) is Absolute, Immutable, and Self-Sufficient. What changes is not God but the manifestation (*tajallī*)—the cosmos that continuously receives divine self-disclosure. The analogy is not organic (God as soul, world as body) but optical (God as Face, world as mirror-image). The image changes; the Face remains untouched.

This preserves both divine intimacy—God is nearer than the jugular vein—and divine transcendence—naught is like unto Him.

On the Ground of Possibility

Whitehead posits "Eternal Objects"—Platonic forms that subsist eternally, waiting to be selected by actual occasions.

These are generic universals: redness, circularity, the number five. God orders them but does not create them.

Participatory Process Monism replaces this with Ibn ʿArabī's Fixed Entities (*al-aʿyān al-thābita*)—the specific, determinate content of divine knowledge. These are not generic potentials but unique archetypes: not "humanness" in general but the immutable identity of each particular human, known by God from eternity. The Fixed Entity of Zayd is not the Fixed Entity of ʿAmr; each has a unique preparedness (*istiʿdād*) that determines what it can receive from divine manifestation.

This transforms the understanding of freedom and destiny. In Whitehead's scheme, actual occasions select among generic possibilities. In Participatory Process Monism, entities fulfill their specific natures—not selecting from a warehouse of parts but actualizing their own eternal truth.

On the Continuity of the Subject

Whitehead's commitment to the epochal nature of actual occasions creates a difficulty: each occasion achieves "satisfaction" and perishes. It loses subjective immediacy—the first-person "I" ceases. What survives is "objective immortality"—the occasion persists as datum, as memory in subsequent occasions and ultimately in God's Consequent Nature. But the experiencing subject, the "I" that felt and loved, is gone.

Participatory Process Monism categorically rejects this annihilation of the subject. Drawing on the concept of the Imaginal Realm (*ʿālam al-mithāl*), it provides robust mechanism for subjective immortality. Death is not the cessation of subjective immediacy but transition to imaginal embodiment within the intermediate realm (*barzakh*). The "I" survives because the "I" was never identical with the physical occasion; it is a ray of divine Spirit (*rūḥ*) traversing worlds.

The soul, understood through Mullā Ṣadrā's doctrine of substantial motion, is not a series of discrete occasions strung together but a continuous substantial reality that intensifies through time. The soul that enters the *barzakh* is the same substantial reality that inhabited the body—now liberated into subtler grades of existence.

DISSOLUTION RATHER THAN SOLUTION

How does Participatory Process Monism address the problems diagnosed in Chapter 2?

It does not solve them in the sense of providing clever answers within the existing framework. It dissolves them by changing the framework in which they arise.

The hard problem asks: how does experience emerge from non-experience? The question presupposes that we start with non-experiential ingredients and must somehow derive experience from them. Participatory Process Monism rejects the presupposition: reality is experiential throughout; the question of emergence from non-experience does not arise.

The measurement problem asks: what causes wave function collapse, and what role does observation play? The question presupposes that observation is external to physical reality, a mysterious intrusion from outside. Participatory Process Monism reframes observation as participation: consciousness does not mysteriously cause collapse; it participates in the actualization that occurs at every moment of becoming.

The meaning crisis asks: how can conscious beings find significance in a universe that has no place for consciousness? The question presupposes that reality is fundamentally meaningless and that meaning must be projected onto it. Participatory Process Monism holds that meaning is woven into reality's fabric—that the cosmos is divine self-disclosure requiring conscious witness for its completion.

None of this makes the problems easy. Explaining how simple experiences integrate into complex ones remains difficult. Understanding exactly how participation works in quantum mechanics is far from complete. Finding one's place in a meaningful cosmos still requires effort and attention. But these are difficulties within a coherent framework rather than impossibilities arising from incoherent assumptions.

WHAT THE FRAMEWORK DOES NOT DO

A responsible account must acknowledge limits. Participatory Process Monism is a philosophical framework, not a scientific theory. It cannot be tested by experiment in the way that quantum mechanics or neuroscience can. It suggests directions for empirical research and provides interpretive frameworks for understanding what science discovers, but it does not generate the kind of precise quantitative predictions that characterize mature physical theories.

The framework does not explain everything. It does not tell us why these particular laws of physics rather than others, why this particular universe rather than some other, why anything at all rather than nothing. These ultimate questions may have no answers—or may have answers that exceed human comprehension.

The combination problem—how simple experiences unite into complex ones—remains a challenge. The framework makes the problem tractable rather than impossible, but tractable is not the same as solved.

And the framework requires accepting something counterintuitive: that experience, in some minimal form, pervades reality, and that even fundamental physical processes have an interior character we cannot directly access. This is not mysticism or magical thinking—it follows from careful analysis of what consciousness requires—but it asks us to expand our sense of what reality includes.

But the alternative, as we have seen, is incoherence: a worldview that cannot explain consciousness, cannot account for observation, cannot ground meaning. The question is not whether to accept some surprising claims but which surprising claims to accept—those that come with principled philosophical justification, or those that leave the most important features of our existence inexplicable.

PART II

THE MONOGRAPHS

SYSTEMATIC PHILOSOPHY

CHAPTER 3

FINDING MEANING BETWEEN MATTER AND MIND — THE ACCESSIBLE INTRODUCTION

You know that you are conscious. Whatever else you might doubt—whether the external world really exists, whether your memories are accurate, whether other people have minds like yours—you cannot doubt this: you are experiencing something right now. There is a felt quality to reading these words, to sitting where you are sitting, to thinking the thoughts you are thinking.

This undeniable fact is the starting point of Finding Meaning Between Matter and Mind, and it is the right starting point. Unlike the other monographs, which presuppose some philosophical background and engage with technical debates, this book begins from what everyone already knows: the simple, immediate reality of conscious experience.

Finding Meaning is designed as the entry point to Hakim

Ibn Adam's philosophical Project. It is shorter than the other monographs, written in accessible prose, and builds its argument step by step from everyday observations rather than academic literature. A reader with no philosophical training can follow it from beginning to end and emerge with a coherent understanding of Participatory Process Monism. This chapter examines how the book accomplishes this—its strategy, its arguments, and its place in the larger Project.

THE STRATEGY

The book's strategy is simple but effective: begin with a puzzle everyone feels, show why the obvious answers fail, and then build an alternative piece by piece.

The puzzle is the mind-body problem, but not presented in technical terms. It is the everyday strangeness of being conscious in a physical world: "You seem to exist in a physical world—a world of matter and energy, of atoms and molecules, of brains and bodies. This physical world appears to follow precise mathematical laws that have nothing to say about consciousness, about experience, about what anything feels like."

How does the felt quality of seeing red relate to the physical processes in the brain? How does the sensation of pain connect to the firing of neurons? These are not questions only philosophers ask. Anyone who has wondered how thoughts can arise from grey matter, or felt the oddness of being an "inner" self looking out at an "outer" world, has felt this puzzle.

The book then examines why the usual answers fail. Materialism—the view that consciousness somehow emerges from purely physical processes—cannot explain how unconscious particles, following physical laws with no reference to experience, suddenly produce experience. "At what point does the light of consciousness switch on? And why?" The question has no answer within the materialist framework, only promissory notes that future science will somehow explain what present science cannot even formulate.

Idealism—the view that consciousness is fundamental and the physical world is dependent on mind—creates different problems. If everything is mental, why is the world so stable? Why do we all experience the same reality? Why does mathematics work so well for predicting physical events? Your imagination is flexible and responsive to your wishes; the physical world is not.

The book's conclusion: "Both views start by assuming that reality must be fundamentally one kind of thing—either unconscious matter or conscious mind—and then struggle to explain how the other appears. What if the problem isn't that we haven't found the right answer? What if the problem is the question itself?"

FOUR KEY INSIGHTS

Having cleared the ground, the book builds its alternative through four interlocking insights. Each chapter develops one insight thoroughly before the next builds upon it.

First insight: Reality is process, not things. The chapter titled "What If Nothing Stays Still?" develops this idea through everyday examples. A flame is not a thing that changes but a process—a continuous transformation of fuel and oxygen into heat and light. A river is not the water but the pattern of flow. You are not the atoms in your body (which are constantly replaced) but the pattern that maintains itself through continuous transformation.

This is not just philosophical speculation. Modern physics supports it. Particles are better understood as excitations in quantum fields—ongoing vibrational patterns—than as tiny solid objects. Organisms are self-maintaining processes, constantly exchanging matter and energy with their environment. "What seems solid and permanent is actually dynamic and temporary—but the patterns can be very long-lasting relative to our timescale, which is why we mistake them for permanent things."

Second insight: Experience goes all the way down. The chapter bearing this title makes the most counterintuitive claim: every process has some form of interior character, some minimal "experience," however, unlike human consciousness.

The argument is simple. If we start with ingredients that have absolutely no experience—zero interiority—then no amount of rearranging can produce experience. You cannot get something from nothing. A trillion unconscious processes do not add up to one conscious moment. But if we start with processes that have minimal interiority, then complex experiences can arise through integration and organization.

The book is careful about what this does and does not mean. "This doesn't mean a quark has thoughts or feelings like ours. It means that a quark's interaction with another quark has an interior aspect—a bare responsiveness, a minimal 'taking account' of the other quark. Not conscious taking account, not deliberate or reflective, but the most primitive form of responsiveness imaginable."

The differences between a quark's "experience" and human consciousness are almost infinite in degree. But they are differences of degree, not kind. This makes consciousness natural rather than miraculous—"not as a miraculous addition to an otherwise dead universe, but as a sophisticated development of something that was there all along in simpler form."

Third insight: Nothing exists alone. The chapter on relationality argues that processes are constituted by their relationships, not merely connected by them. A tree seems independent, but it exists through relationships with soil fungi, atmospheric carbon dioxide, sunlight, pollinators. Remove these relationships and you do not have an independent tree; you have a dead tree.

This is even clearer in physics. Quantum particles do not have definite properties until they interact. Position and momentum are not pre-existing attributes waiting to be discovered; they emerge from interaction. Relationships come first; properties emerge.

Human consciousness exhibits the same relational character. A concept like "tall" has no meaning except in relation to a context. Relationships constitute your identity—with your past, your environment, and other people. "What something is depends fundamentally on what it's related to."

Fourth insight: Knowing is participation. The chapter "You Help Make What You See" develops the final piece. Observation is not passive reception but active engagement. Quantum mechanics shows this starkly: the act of measurement affects what state a system is in. But everyday experience confirms it too. Attention shapes what appears in consciousness. Questions determine what answers are available. Different modes of engagement reveal different aspects of reality.

This is not subjectivism—the book is emphatic about this. "Reality pushes back. You can't walk through walls by believing you can." The world has structure that exists independently of what anyone thinks. But which aspects of that structure become manifest depends on how you engage with it. "The patterns and regularities of reality are revealed through interaction, and different modes of interaction reveal different patterns."

PUTTING IT TOGETHER

The book's final chapters synthesize the four insights into a unified picture. Reality is ongoing process, fundamentally relational, with both exterior structure (what physics describes) and interior character (what experience reveals). Mind and matter are not separate realms but different perspectives on the same processes. Knowing is participatory—you are not outside reality looking in but part of reality becoming aware of itself.

This picture dissolves the puzzles that motivated the inquiry. The hard problem of consciousness—how does experience arise from non-experience?—dissolves when experience is recognized as fundamental rather than emergent. The explanatory gap between physical description and felt quality—why should certain neural processes feel like anything?—dissolves when physical and experiential descriptions are recognized as exterior and interior perspectives on the same process. The measurement problem in physics—what role does observation play?—becomes less paradoxical when observation is understood as participation rather than passive registration.

The book acknowledges what remains mysterious. The combination problem—how do simple experiences integrate into complex ones?—is not fully solved. The specific relationship between brain organization and conscious experience is not explained in detail. The framework provides conceptual orientation, not complete answers. But the puzzles are now tractable rather than impossible. We know the direction of inquiry even if we have not reached the destination.

THE DIFFERENCE IT MAKES

The book's final chapter asks what practical difference this understanding makes. The answer is that it changes how we experience ourselves and our place in reality.

If consciousness is a fluke—an accident in an otherwise dead universe—then we are fundamentally alien to reality, "a ghost in a machine, an awareness trapped in unconscious matter, forever separate from the world you observe." But if consciousness is natural, a development of something fundamental, then we belong. "You're not alien to reality—you're part of it. Your awareness, your experience, your choices—these aren't anomalies. They're reality becoming conscious of itself, participating in its own ongoing creativity."

This changes how we relate to nature. Instead of seeing the natural world as dead resources, we recognize it as process with its own forms of interiority. This changes how we think about other people—not as separate minds behind barriers of skin but as fellow participants in relational, experiential reality. This changes how we think about knowledge—not detached observation but participatory engagement where our mode of approach matters for what is revealed.

And it changes how we think about meaning. "You're not an isolated observer watching reality unfold. You're a participant in an ongoing creative process. Your choices, your attention, your relationships—all of these are ways the universe becomes conscious of itself and shapes its own future."

THE BOOK'S DISTINCTIVE CONTRIBUTION

Finding Meaning Between Matter and Mind is not merely a simplified version of the other monographs. It makes its own distinctive contribution to the Project.

Accessibility as philosophical achievement. Making complex ideas genuinely accessible without distorting them is itself a significant accomplishment. The book demonstrates that Participatory Process Monism can be explained to anyone willing to follow an argument, that it does not require technical background, that it connects with questions people already have.

Emphasis on lived implications. More than any other work in the Project, this book emphasizes what the philosophical framework means for how we live. The chapter on "What This Means" draws out implications for understanding consciousness, science, agency, value, relationships, and our place in reality. The philosophy is not merely intellectually satisfying; it is existentially transformative.

Direct engagement with common sense. The book takes seriously the common-sense view that matter is "stuff" and consciousness is rare. It explains exactly why this view fails and exactly how the alternative resolves its problems. This direct engagement makes the book useful for readers who have not yet encountered the puzzles in their sharpest form.

Connection to contemplative practice. More than the other monographs, Finding Meaning suggests that understanding can be verified through direct experience. The participatory character of knowing can be confirmed by attending to how attention shapes experience, how questions shape answers, how engagement reveals different aspects of reality. The book invites readers not just to understand but to see.

READING RECOMMENDATIONS

For readers new to Hakim Ibn Adam's work, Finding Meaning Between Matter and Mind is the natural starting point. It requires no background, builds systematically, and provides the conceptual framework that the other works presuppose.

After Finding Meaning, readers might take different paths. Those interested in the theoretical foundations can turn to An Inquiry into First Principles for the full epistemological framework. Those drawn to the theological dimensions can turn to Naught Is Like Unto Him for the Islamic philosophical background. Those interested in historical precedents can turn to Knowledge Coordination

Patterns for case studies in integration.

The fiction requires the philosophical framework to resonate fully. A reader who has absorbed Finding Meaning will understand why the protagonist of The Divided Light experiences the cell's hesitation as more than chemistry, why the Mitochondrion of The Ancient Bargain speaks of continuous creation and the Breath of the Merciful, why the question "What is it like to be?" structures the dialogue between human and AI. The framework is not imposed on the fiction; the fiction explores what the framework means when lived.

THE INVITATION

The book ends with an invitation rather than a conclusion:

"We don't ask you to believe what we've said. We ask you to consider it, to test it against your own experience, to see if it helps you understand yourself and your world more deeply. Philosophy isn't about accepting doctrines—it's about thinking clearly about questions that matter. The questions about consciousness, about your place in nature, about the relationship between what you experience and what science describes—these questions will continue to draw you. We've offered one set of answers. The thinking is yours to do."

This tone—inviting rather than dogmatic, provisional rather than final, pointing toward further inquiry rather than closing questions—characterizes the entire Project. Finding Meaning Between Matter and Mind offers the clearest expression of this philosophical stance: confident enough to present a coherent vision, humble enough to acknowledge its limits, honest enough to admit that the thinking ultimately belongs to the reader.

CHAPTER 4

AN INQUIRY INTO FIRST PRINCIPLES

The largest and most ambitious work of the Project, *An Inquiry into First Principles* runs to twenty chapters. It is subtitled "Toward Conscious Participation in an Unfolding Reality"—a phrase that announces both its method and its conclusion. The book argues that the search for foundational truths is not an abstract exercise in logic-chopping but a form of participation in reality's ongoing self-disclosure. To inquire into first principles is to engage in an activity that transforms the inquirer.

This chapter maps the monograph's terrain, identifies its central arguments, and demonstrates how it establishes the epistemological groundwork for the rest of the Project.

WHAT THE BOOK ATTEMPTS

Every discipline rests on assumptions it does not itself justify. Physics assumes that nature behaves according to mathematical laws discoverable through observation and experiment—but physics cannot prove this assumption without circular reasoning. Philosophy assumes that logical analysis yields reliable knowledge—but this assumption cannot be established by logical analysis alone without begging the question. Religion assumes that revelation provides access to truths beyond ordinary inquiry—but this assumption requires criteria for distinguishing genuine revelation from delusion, criteria that cannot come from revelation itself.

These are not embarrassing secrets that professionals hide from outsiders. They are structural features of any systematic inquiry. To know anything, we must start somewhere. But wherever we start, we can always ask: why *there*? Why *those* assumptions rather than others?

An Inquiry *into First Principles* takes this problem seriously rather than dismissing it or pretending it does not exist. The book's central claim is that foundational commitments can be surfaced, examined, and evaluated through systematic comparison—not by finding some neutral standpoint outside all traditions (which does not exist), but by bringing different approaches into principled dialogue and testing them against shared criteria.

The criteria the book proposes are: **coherence** (does the framework contradict itself?), **explanatory scope** (how much does it illuminate?), **depth** (does it engage fundamental structures or only surface phenomena?), **fruitfulness** (does it generate new insights and research programs?), and **existential adequacy** (does it orient human action and provide resources for living well?). No single criterion is decisive; frameworks must be evaluated holistically, and reasonable people may weigh the criteria differently. But the criteria provide a basis for rational comparison that avoids both dogmatism ("my tradition is simply right and yours is simply wrong") and relativism ("all perspectives are equally valid, so inquiry is pointless").

THE TRIADIC METHOD

The book's most distinctive contribution is its articulation of what it calls the "triadic methodology"—the claim that human inquiry has historically proceeded along three primary pathways, each offering distinct but complementary access to truth.

The empirical path involves disciplined attention to phenomena through observation, measurement, and experimental manipulation. This is the domain of the natural sciences, where hypotheses are tested against sensory evidence, and theories are refined based on predictive success. The empirical path excels at discovering patterns and regularities in the physical world; it has given us modern medicine, technology, and our understanding of cosmic evolution. Its limitation is that it cannot justify its own foundations: it cannot empirically test the assumption that empirical testing is reliable, nor can it determine the values that guide research or the meanings that make findings significant.

The rational path involves conceptual analysis, logical inference, and examination of the criteria governing explanation itself. This is the domain of philosophy and mathematics, where coherence and necessity matter more than sensory observation. The rational path reveals what must be true for any coherent account of reality—the principle of non-contradiction, the structure of valid inference, the conditions for the possibility of experience. Its limitation is that it cannot by itself determine what actually exists; pure reason cannot settle whether the universe contains one substance or many, whether time is real or illusory, whether God exists or not.

The revelatory path encompasses the domains of meaning disclosed through conscience, symbol, scripture, and transformative experience—those moments when communities claim access to moral and metaphysical insight not derivable from observation or analysis alone. This is the domain of religious and spiritual traditions, where participation rather than detachment is the mode of knowing. The revelatory path addresses questions that the other paths handle only obliquely: the meaning of suffering, hope beyond death, ultimate purpose, the ground of moral obligation. Its limitation is that revelatory claims are contested, interpretation is required, and criteria for distinguishing authentic from inauthentic spiritual experience are themselves debatable.

The book's central methodological wager is that these three approaches need not remain isolated in disciplinary silos. They can be brought into principled dialogue, with each correcting and complementing the other. Empirical findings constrain philosophical speculation (we cannot coherently hold views contradicted by well-established observation). Rational analysis clarifies the structure of empirical claims (we must understand what we are asserting before we can test it). Revelatory traditions raise questions that neither observation nor analysis generates on its own (questions about meaning and value that orient the entire inquiry). The dialogue is not a merger that erases distinctions but a conversation that respects differences while seeking convergence where it can be honestly found.

THE ARCHITECTURE OF THE BOOK

The twenty chapters are organized into six parts, each addressing a distinct aspect of the foundational inquiry while contributing to the cumulative argument.

Part I (Chapters 1–3) establishes the philosophical framework. Chapter 1 asks what first principles are and why they matter, tracing the history of foundational thinking from ancient Greece through contemporary science and noting its persistence across domains from mathematics to business strategy to spiritual practice. Chapter 2 confronts the "problem of foundation"—the paradoxes of infinite regress and circularity that threaten any foundational project. If every claim requires justification, and justification requires further claims, we face either an infinite regress (which never terminates) or a circle (which assumes what it seeks to prove). Chapter 3 introduces the triadic methodology as a response: not a solution that eliminates the problem but a strategy for living productively with foundational uncertainty through mutual correction among complementary approaches.

Part II (Chapters 4–6) examines first principles within physics and cosmology. Chapter 4 analyzes the laws of physics—conservation principles, thermodynamics, quantum mechanics, relativity—asking what kind of necessity they possess and what they reveal about reality's structure. Chapter 5 turns to mathematical foundations, engaging debates about set theory, logical pluralism, Gödel's incompleteness theorems, and the "unreasonable effectiveness of mathematics" in describing the physical world. Chapter 6 addresses cosmological questions: the Big Bang, fine-tuning, multiverse theories, and the ultimate origin problem that science approaches but cannot resolve on its own terms.

Part III (Chapters 7–10) develops the conceptual apparatus necessary for rigorous comparison across domains. Chapter 7 examines the certainty of existence— the Cartesian starting point and its contemporary reassessment. Chapter 8 surveys theories of being (ontology): substance versus process, materialism versus idealism, the mind-body problem. Chapter 9 analyzes the structure of knowledge (epistemology): empiricism versus rationalism, foundationalism versus coherentism, the problem of induction, virtue epistemology. Chapter 10 addresses logical foundations: the classical laws of thought, alternative logics, the relationship between logic and reality. These chapters provide the technical vocabulary and conceptual distinctions necessary for the comparative work to come.

Part IV (Chapters 11–14) engages religious and moral dimensions. Chapter 11 examines the phenomenology of the sacred—Rudolf Otto's analysis of the numinous, mystical experience across traditions, the question of whether religious awareness constitutes a genuine mode of knowing. Chapter 12 surveys creation narratives and concepts of ultimate reality across traditions: the Abrahamic model of creation *ex nihilo*, Hindu cosmology, Buddhist dependent origination, indigenous perspectives. Chapter 13 addresses revelation and authority: the nature of prophetic communication, the formation of scripture, the relationship between faith and reason, criteria for assessing revelatory claims. Chapter 14 examines moral first principles: whether moral truths are objective or constructed, the sources of moral knowledge, the universality or particularity of ethical principles.

Part V (Chapters 15–17) undertakes comparative evaluation of major worldviews. Chapter 15 asks "Where Science, Philosophy, and Religion Meet"—identifying convergence points around intelligibility, consciousness, and fine-tuning. Chapter 16 examines "Competing Worldviews"—naturalistic materialism, theistic realism, idealism, process philosophy, Eastern non-dualism—testing each against the evaluative criteria developed earlier. Chapter 17 addresses "The Unity of Truth"—whether the convergence thesis can be sustained, how to handle persistent tensions, and what methodological principles enable productive integration without forced synthesis.

Part VI (Chapters 18–20) turns to practical implications. Chapter 18, "Living with First Principles," examines how foundational commitments shape decision-making, moral psychology, responses to suffering and mortality. Chapter 19, "The Ongoing Quest," acknowledges that foundational questions remain open, that inquiry is never complete, that the search itself constitutes a form of participation in reality's self-disclosure. Chapter 20, the conclusion, articulates provisional affirmations about what the inquiry has established while preserving appropriate humility about what remains unknown.

KEY ARGUMENTS

Several arguments recur throughout the monograph, forming its conceptual spine.

Against the warfare metaphor. Popular discourse perpetuates the idea that science and religion are inherently at war—that accepting one requires rejecting the other. The book systematically dismantles this narrative. The "warfare thesis" rests on historical misunderstandings (the Galileo affair was more complex than the myth suggests; many scientific pioneers were devoutly religious; the very concepts of "science" and "religion" as distinct domains emerged only in the modern period). More fundamentally, the thesis assumes that empirical and revelatory claims compete for the same territory, which they need not. Science asks how things happen; religion asks why they matter. The answers can conflict only if one domain overreaches into the other's territory—as when young-earth creationism makes empirical claims about geology, or when eliminative materialism makes metaphysical claims about the unreality of consciousness.

Against reductive materialism. The book argues that materialist reductionism—the view that everything real is ultimately physical, and that consciousness, meaning, and value are either illusory or reducible to physical processes—cannot coherently account for its own conditions of possibility. The scientist who claims that only physical facts are real is making a metaphysical claim that cannot itself be established by physical investigation. The philosopher who argues that consciousness is an illusion is using consciousness to make the argument. The claim that meaning is merely subjective projection presupposes a meaningful distinction between projection and reality. Reductive materialism, consistently applied, undermines the very inquiry that produces it.

For epistemic humility. The book repeatedly emphasizes that foundational inquiry does not terminate in certainty. Gödel's incompleteness theorems demonstrate that any formal system rich enough to express arithmetic contains truths it cannot prove—a result with implications extending far beyond mathematics. The problem of induction (how can past regularities justify expectations about the future?) has no conclusive solution. The criteria for evaluating worldviews are themselves debatable. This does not mean that all views are equally valid or that inquiry is pointless; it means that inquiry proceeds with appropriate humility, holding conclusions provisionally, remaining open to revision, recognizing that the quest itself may be more important than any final answer.

For convergent truth. Despite irreducible differences among traditions and disciplines, the book argues that genuine convergence is possible and significant when it occurs. When physics, philosophy, and contemplative traditions independently point toward similar insights—about the observer-participatory structure of reality, about the inadequacy of substance metaphysics, about the primacy of relation over isolated existence—this convergence provides evidence that something real is being disclosed. Convergence does not prove truth (multiple traditions might converge on error), but it provides confirmation that strengthens confidence beyond what any single approach could achieve alone.

HOW THE MONOGRAPH GROUNDS THE PROJECT

An Inquiry into First Principles functions as the epistemological foundation for the entire Project. It establishes:

The legitimacy of the triadic method. The works of fiction draw on scientific observation, philosophical analysis, and contemplative insight without apology. *An Inquiry into First Principles* justifies this integration by arguing that no single mode of knowing is sufficient and that their combination is not arbitrary eclecticism but a methodologically necessary one.

The criteria for evaluation. When the fiction dramatizes competing views—mechanism versus meaning in *The Divided Light*, digital versus analog in *The Ancient Bargain*—the monograph provides the conceptual apparatus for assessing them. We are not simply offered perspectives but frameworks that can be tested for coherence, scope, depth, fruitfulness, and existential adequacy.

The limits of the inquiry. The monograph's insistence on epistemic humility extends to the fiction, which rejects easy resolutions. The protagonist of *Not About Nothing* cannot answer whether his choices were worth their cost. The dialogue in *The Ancient Bargain* does not resolve; it continues. This is not authorial evasion but philosophical honesty: some questions remain genuinely open.

The participatory stance. The subtitle of *An Inquiry into First Principles*—"Toward Conscious Participation in an Unfolding Reality"—announces what the fiction will embody. Inquiry is not the extraction of facts from an external world but participation in reality's ongoing self-disclosure. *The inquiry transforms the inquirer.* This theme, stated abstractly in the monograph, becomes vivid in the novellas, where the protagonist's investigation of consciousness transforms his own consciousness.

READING RECOMMENDATIONS

An Inquiry into First Principles is the longest and most demanding of the monographs. Readers approaching from different backgrounds may benefit from various entry points:

Those with scientific training might begin with Part II (physics and cosmology), which engages material they will find familiar while revealing its philosophical implications. From there, Part III (conceptual apparatus) and Part V (worldview comparison) develop the framework, with Part

I (methodology) providing retrospective clarity about what the earlier chapters were doing.

Those with philosophical training should begin with Part I (methodology) and Part III (conceptual apparatus), which articulate the book's distinctive approach before testing it against scientific and religious material.

Those with religious or theological backgrounds might enter through Part IV (religious dimensions), which treats revelatory claims with intellectual seriousness while maintaining critical standards. The earlier parts then provide the philosophical scaffolding for that treatment.

Those primarily interested in the fiction might read Chapter 1 (why first principles matter) and Chapter 3 (the triadic method) for orientation, then proceed directly to the novellas, returning to the monograph as questions arise.

However one approaches it, *An Inquiry into First Principles* rewards patience. It is not light reading. But it provides the intellectual architecture within which the other works make their most profound sense.

CHAPTER 5

KNOWLEDGE COORDINATION PATTERNS — TWELVE HISTORICAL EXPERIMENTS

How do you bring different ways of knowing into productive dialogue without forcing a false unity or abandoning the rigour that makes each valuable?

This is the question that *Knowledge Coordination Patterns* addresses—not through abstract theorizing but through careful examination of twelve historical figures who attempted various forms of synthesis across disciplinary and cultural boundaries. The book's subtitle announces its method: "Twelve Historical Experiments in Interdisciplinary Coordination." These are not heroes to be emulated or sages dispensing timeless wisdom. They are case studies—some successful within their contexts, others instructive failures—from which contemporary readers might extract transferable practices and cautionary lessons.

This monograph is the most methodologically self-conscious of the Project. It explicitly resists the romantic narrative of lost unity and modern fragmentation. It acknowledges its own limitations and selection biases. It maintains throughout a tone of critical assessment rather than celebration. If *An Inquiry into First Principles* argues for the possibility of integration and *Naught Is Like Unto Him* demonstrates the intellectual riches of a particular tradition, *Knowledge Coordination Patterns* asks the harder question: how has integration actually been attempted, and what can we learn from both the successes and the failures?

THE PROBLEM REFRAMED

The book begins by reframing the problem of knowledge fragmentation. Popular discourse often treats specialization as a symptom of cultural decline—as if there were once a golden age of unified wisdom from which we have fallen. This narrative is historically naive. What appeared to be unity in earlier periods often masked exclusions (of women, non-elite classes, and non-Western traditions) and power dynamics (whose synthesis is imposed on whom?) rather than genuine intellectual achievement.

The monograph proposes a more modest and precise definition of the problem. Knowledge fragmentation is not a civilizational pathology but an observable set of interface difficulties: the divergence of technical vocabularies that makes translation costly, the incompatibility of data standards that impedes sharing, the institutional incentives that penalize boundary-crossing work, and the power asymmetries that privilege specific disciplines in policy discussions. These are design problems, not existential crises. They admit of practical solutions—though not easy ones.

The question, then, is not whether specialization represents a decline but where coordination failures genuinely impede progress on problems that matter. Climate change, pandemic response, and technological governance—these require orchestrating insights across multiple domains without sacrificing the rigour that makes specialized knowledge valuable. The historical case studies are examined not for timeless principles but for transferable practices: what worked, what failed, under what conditions, and why.

THE TWELVE FIGURES

The book examines twelve figures across eight chapters, organized both roughly chronologically and thematically.

Chapter 2: Pythagoras and Plato. The ancient Greeks pioneered coordination through mathematical structure. Pythagoras and his followers discovered that musical harmony, geometric proportion, and numerical relationships exhibited deep correspondences—the same ratios that produced consonant intervals on a string also appeared in planetary orbits and geometric forms. This was not mystical numerology but genuine pattern recognition: mathematics as a coordination language across domains.

Plato systematized this insight through his theory of Forms and his "Divided Line" epistemology, which organized different modes of knowing (conjecture, belief, understanding, dialectical knowledge) into a hierarchical framework. The book credits these innovations while noting their limitations: the theory of Forms faces well-known metaphysical problems, the hierarchical organization embeds value judgments, and the exclusion of empirical observation as a source of genuine knowledge would prove a lasting liability.

Chapter 3: Avicenna and al-Bīrūnī. The Islamic Golden Age produced two contrasting approaches to coordination. Avicenna (Ibn Sīnā) developed a systematic philosophical architecture, using the essence-existence distinction as a coordinating tool to analyze how particulars relate to general categories. His hierarchical emanationist framework organized knowledge from the Necessary Existent down through the intelligences to the material world.

Al-Bīrūnī adopted a different approach: an empirical-comparative approach. His work on India involved linguistic immersion, cultural translation, and the development of comparative matrices for analyzing different civilizations. Where Avicenna built hierarchical systems, al-Bīrūnī built networks of careful comparison. The book treats both as valuable models with different strengths: systematic organization versus empirical sensitivity, vertical hierarchy versus lateral connection.

Chapter 4: Aquinas and Leonardo. Medieval and Renaissance Europe produced its own experiments. Aquinas developed the "disputed question" method—a procedural coordination that brought opposing positions into structured dialogue—and his doctrine of analogical predication provided a way to speak meaningfully across ontological levels (from creatures to God) without collapsing distinctions. His natural law theory coordinated theological, philosophical, and practical domains.

Leonardo represents a different mode: empirical-aesthetic coordination through visual investigation. His *"sapere vedere"* (knowing how to see) made disciplined observation the foundation for coordinating anatomy, engineering, art, and natural philosophy. His notebooks embody a network rather than a hierarchy—lateral connections between domains rather than vertical organization.

Chapter 5: Leibniz and Goethe. The Enlightenment produced two ambitious projects that both failed instructively. Leibniz pursued formal coordination through his *characteristica universalis*—a universal symbolic language that would reduce reasoning to calculation and enable coordination across all domains through shared notation. His monadological metaphysics attempted to coordinate mind and matter, physics and theology, through a single systematic framework.

Goethe pursued phenomenological coordination through his morphological method—tracing the transformation of fundamental forms (the "Urpflanze," the archetypal plant) across variations. His "delicate empiricism" combined sensory observation with imaginative participation, refusing the separation of subject and object that characterized the emerging scientific method.

Both failed. Leibniz's universal language was never completed; his metaphysics proved more influential as provocation than as solution. Physicists rejected Goethe's colour theory; his morphological insights were absorbed into evolutionary biology but stripped of their philosophical framework. The book examines why: theoretical overreach, institutional resistance, and the difficulty of sustaining individual synthesis projects across generations.

Chapter 6: Teilhard de Chardin and Muhammad Iqbal. The twentieth century produced ambitious attempts to coordinate evolutionary science with religious thought. Teilhard, the Jesuit paleontologist, proposed that evolution exhibits directionality toward increasing complexity and consciousness, culminating in the "Omega Point"—a cosmic convergence that he identified with Christ.

Iqbal, the Muslim philosopher-poet, developed an evolutionary theism in which divine creative action operates through evolutionary processes. His concept of "dynamic selfhood" proposed that consciousness at all levels participates in cosmic creativity.

The book's assessment is critical. Both thinkers assumed orthogenesis—directed evolution toward predetermined goals—which conflicts with the Darwinian understanding of evolution as non-teleological. Their syntheses were religiously motivated attempts to restore purpose and direction to a universe that biology reveals to be undirected.

The coordination failed because it distorted the science to fit the theology. Yet both raised questions that remain important: how to understand consciousness in evolutionary terms, how to coordinate scientific and religious frameworks without distorting either.

Chapter 7: Jung and Bohm. The final case studies examine two twentieth-century figures whose attempts at coordination remain influential yet problematic. Jung's analytical psychology sought to integrate clinical observation with mythology, religion, and physics through concepts such as the collective unconscious and synchronicity. His clinical methods were empirically grounded; his theoretical extensions were not. The collective unconscious may be more parsimoniously explained through cognitive biases and cultural transmission than through metaphysical postulates. Synchronicity remains unvalidated as anything more than a meaningful coincidence interpreted through confirmation bias.

Bohm's physics presents a similar pattern. His de Broglie-Bohm interpretation of quantum mechanics is a legitimate scientific theory—a deterministic alternative to the Copenhagen interpretation that makes the same predictions. But his "implicate order"—a speculative framework in which all parts are enfolded within each other—is metaphysics, not physics. It makes no testable predictions beyond standard quantum mechanics. His dialogue method for group communication, while practically influential, lacks rigorous validation compared to other facilitation approaches.

The book's lesson: convergence in vocabulary does not establish convergence in theory. That Jung and Bohm both used holistic language does not mean their frameworks coordinate at any deep level. Apparent synthesis may mask category errors.

FOUR HEURISTIC PRINCIPLES

From these case studies, the book extracts four patterns that recur across different contexts. It treats these explicitly as heuristic principles—working hypotheses rather than established laws—and devotes careful attention to counterexamples and limitations.

Multi-Dimensional Epistemology (MDE). The historical figures typically coordinated multiple sources of knowledge rather than relying exclusively on single modes: empirical observation, logical analysis, intuitive insight, textual interpretation, and experiential engagement. This aligns with the triadic methodology developed in *An Inquiry into First Principles.*

However, the book notes counterexamples. Logical positivism achieved valuable clarifications through a single-mode focus on empirical verification. Pure mathematics generates insights through abstract reasoning divorced from empirical application. The apparent prevalence of multi-dimensional approaches in the sample may reflect selection bias.

Hierarchical-Organic Organization (HOO). Many figures organize knowledge into levels that maintain organic rather than merely aggregative relationships—higher levels emerging from, but not reducible to, lower levels, with both upward and downward causal influences. Aquinas's participation metaphysics exemplifies this: each level participates analogically in higher levels while maintaining its proper perfection.

But again, counterexamples exist. Network theories, rhizomatic philosophies, and Indigenous knowledge systems achieve coordination through lateral connections rather than vertical stratification. The prevalence of hierarchy in the sample may reflect historical and cultural biases rather than functional necessity.

Process-Relational Ontology (PRO). Several figures emphasize process, temporality, and relational constitution over substance metaphysics—treating entities as relatively stable patterns within flux rather than independent objects with intrinsic properties. This aligns with Participatory Process Monism.

Yet Parmenides and Spinoza achieved sophisticated syntheses while emphasizing permanence over process. Mathematical Platonism integrates diverse domains through timeless abstract objects. Process thinking appears particularly valuable for developmental and evolutionary phenomena, but less necessary for logical systems and mathematical structures.

Participatory Consciousness (PC). Many figures treat knowledge as emerging through participatory engagement between knower and known rather than detached observation. Plotinus's *henosis*, Sufi ma'rifa, Goethe's "exact sensorial imagination"—all involve the co-constitution of subject and object through the knowing act.

But formal coordination through systematic abstraction often works best when minimizing subjective participation. Claims about participatory knowledge face particular validation challenges: first-person reports of transformative knowing are phenomenologically interesting but challenging to compare rigorously with non-participatory approaches.

The book's conclusion: these principles deserve investigation precisely because they appear across different contexts, but their apparent universality may reflect selection bias, cultural narrowness, or interpretive projection. Selective rather than comprehensive deployment often proves most effective. Climate science benefits from multi-dimensional coordination and process thinking, but may not require hierarchical organization or participatory consciousness.

Coordination Without Unification

The book's most crucial methodological contribution is its

reframing of the goal. The aim is not metaphysical unity—a single framework that encompasses all knowledge—but coordination: "the creation of durable coordination mechanisms between heterogeneous knowledge communities."

This is interface design rather than system building. It involves developing shared "boundary objects" (datasets, standards, conceptual bridges) that enable communication without forcing homogenization. It requires "minimal ontologies" that allow interoperation while preserving methodological diversity. It demands governance frameworks that protect different ways of knowing while enabling joint action on shared problems.

The reframing has practical implications. Some domains may be irreducibly different. Forced synthesis often produces neither good science nor good philosophy. Apparent unity in earlier periods frequently masked exclusions rather than genuine achievement. Effective coordination sometimes requires accepting productive tensions rather than resolving them prematurely.

This is not relativism. The book maintains that some coordination attempts succeed and others fail, that criteria exist for evaluating them, that genuine progress is possible. But success means functional coordination for particular purposes, not final synthesis that closes all questions.

THE MONOGRAPH'S PLACE IN THE PROJECT

Knowledge Coordination Patterns provides the methodological self-reflection that the other works presuppose. *An Inquiry into First Principles* argues for triadic methodology; this monograph shows what triadic coordination has looked like historically—its achievements and its failures. *Naught Is Like Unto Him* presents Islamic theology as a resource; this monograph examines Avicenna and al-Bīrūnī as specific coordination experiments within that tradition, noting both what they achieved and what they excluded.

The fiction, too, benefits from this background. *The Ancient Bargain* stages a coordination problem—how do Ribosome and Mitochondrion, with their different "languages" (digital and analog, event and flow), achieve collaboration? The dialogue form itself is a coordination mechanism, a boundary object that enables communication without forcing identity. The lesson of *Knowledge Coordination Patterns*—that productive coordination may require maintaining tension rather than resolving it— illuminates why the drama refuses synthesis, why the final word is "Continue."

HONEST LIMITATIONS

The book is unusually explicit about its own limitations. Twelve figures from primarily Western and Islamic traditions cannot establish universal patterns. Many represent elite male perspectives from particular institutional contexts. Alternative knowledge traditions— Indigenous, African, East Asian—receive insufficient attention. The selection of recognized "integrators" may create circular reasoning about what coordination looks like.

The book also brackets certain contemporary claims. While coordination problems are real, attributing widespread cultural anxieties primarily to academic specialization lacks robust evidence. Multiple social determinants—economic inequality, political instability, technological disruption—likely matter more than disciplinary boundaries for understanding contemporary psychological distress.

This honesty is itself methodologically important. A book about coordination that claimed more than it could establish would undermine its own project. The acknowledgment of limits models the epistemic humility that genuine coordination requires.

CHAPTER 6

NAUGHT IS LIKE UNTO HIM — DIVINE TRANSCENDENCE IN ISLAMIC THOUGHT

The title comes from a Quranic verse: *laysa kamithlihi shay'un* — "There is nothing like unto Him" (42:11). This phrase, seven words in Arabic, has generated over a millennium of theological reflection. How can we speak of a God who exceeds all speech? How can we know what transcends all knowing? How can finite minds approach the Infinite without reducing it to their own measure?

Naught Is Like Unto Him is the Project's most explicitly theological monograph. It traces how Muslim thinkers across fourteen centuries have grappled with divine incomparability—not as an abstract puzzle but as the fundamental condition of authentic religious thought. The book argues that this tradition offers resources urgently needed by contemporary philosophy: sophisticated frameworks for thinking about that which exceeds conceptual grasp without collapsing into silence or skepticism.

THE CENTRAL PARADOX

The Quran presents a God who is utterly transcendent yet intimately present. The same scripture that declares "nothing is like unto Him" also affirms that He is "nearer than the jugular vein" (50:16). The same revelation that insists on divine incomparability also names God with ninety-nine names—the Merciful, the Knowing, the Powerful, the Living—names that seem to attribute qualities we also find in creatures.

This is the paradox at the heart of Islamic theology. God must be affirmed (we can speak meaningfully of Him) yet negated (nothing we say captures His reality). The names are true (God really is Merciful, really is Knowing) yet their meaning when applied to God differs entirely from their meaning when applied to creatures. As an early authority put it: "The sharing is in utterance only, not in meaning. When we say Allah is 'knowing' and humans are 'knowing,' only the word is shared. The reality differs more than the distance between heaven and earth—rather, no comparison exists at all."

This is not a problem to be solved but a tension to be maintained. The monograph traces how different schools of Islamic thought have maintained it—some emphasizing transcendence to the point of near-silence, others emphasizing affirmation to the point of anthropomorphism, most seeking a middle path that preserves both poles without collapsing either.

THE ARCHITECTURE OF THE BOOK

Naught Is Like Unto Him spans twenty-four chapters organized into five parts.

Part I (Chapters 1–4) establishes foundations. Chapter 1 examines the Quranic verse itself—its linguistic structure (the emphatic double negation), its context (following immediately after affirmations of divine creative power), and the earliest interpretations by the Prophet's Companions and their successors. Chapter 2 surveys divine names in Quran and Hadith, noting how the names seem to pull in opposite directions: some emphasizing transcendence (the Holy, the Exalted), others suggesting relation (the Merciful, the Near). Chapter 3 traces early debates about theological language—whether the names are eternal or created, whether attributes shared with creatures imply similarity. Chapter 4 examines how revelation, interpretation, and mystery interact in classical Islamic hermeneutics.

Part II (Chapters 5–8) surveys the major theological schools. Chapter 5 presents the Ash'arite contribution—the dominant Sunni school that developed the methodology of *bilā kayf* ("without asking how"): affirming what scripture affirms while refusing to specify the manner of divine attributes. Chapter 6 examines Mu'tazilite rationalism—an earlier school that emphasized divine unity so strongly that it denied real distinctions among divine attributes, treating the names as human descriptions rather than divine realities. Chapter 7 presents the Maturidite synthesis—a school that mediated between Ash'arite and Mu'tazilite positions. Chapter 8 traces the development of apophatic theology (*tanzīh*)—the tradition of negative theology that approaches God through systematic negation of creaturely categories.

Part III (Chapters 9–12) engages the philosophical tradition. Chapter 9 examines al-Ghazali's integration of philosophy with traditional theology—his critique of the philosophers on certain points while incorporating their methods on others. Chapter 10 presents Ibn Sina's concept of the "Necessary Existent"—a rigorously philosophical approach to divine transcendence that influenced all subsequent Islamic thought. Chapter 11 explores

Suhrawardi's Illuminationism—a light metaphysics that made transcendence luminously present rather than abstractly distant. Chapter 12 examines Mulla Sadra's dynamic metaphysics—the doctrine of "substantial motion" that transformed substance philosophy into process ontology.

Part IV (Chapters 13–18) turns to the mystical tradition. Chapter 13 introduces the "Unity of Being" (*wahdat al-wujūd*)—the controversial doctrine associated with Ibn Arabi that all existence is divine self-disclosure. Chapter 14 examines Ibn Arabi's theory of divine self-manifestation (*tajallī*)—how the Hidden Treasure loved to be known and breathed the cosmos into existence. Chapter 15 explores how mystical theology handles apparently contradictory divine names (the Manifest and the Hidden, the First and the Last). Chapter 16 discusses perpetual creation (*khalq jadīd*)—the doctrine that the world is recreated each moment through continuous divine activity. Chapter 17 surveys broader Sufi approaches to transcendence. Chapter 18 contextualizes the "ecstatic utterances" (*shatahiyyāt*)—those startling statements by mystics in states of spiritual intoxication that seem to transgress the boundaries of orthodox theology.

Part V (Chapters 19–24) addresses contemporary implications. These chapters bring the classical tradition into dialogue with modern philosophy, examining what Islamic theology offers to current debates about religious language, the limits of reason, and the possibility of speaking meaningfully about that which exceeds all categories.

KEY CONCEPTS

Several concepts recur throughout the monograph, forming its conceptual vocabulary.

Tanzīh and Tashbīh. These Arabic terms name the two poles of the theological paradox. *Tanzīh* (from a root meaning "to declare pure" or "to remove") refers to the negation of creaturely attributes from God—declaring Him free of all likeness to creation. *Tashbīh* (from a root meaning "to liken" or "to compare") refers to the affirmation of attributes that seem to make God similar to creatures—affirming that He truly is Merciful, Knowing, Powerful.

Pure *tanzīh* leads to a God so transcendent that nothing can be said of Him—a philosophical abstraction rather than the living God of scripture and experience. Pure *tashbīh* leads to anthropomorphism—a God made in our image, reduced to creaturely categories. The task of theology is to maintain both simultaneously: affirming what scripture affirms (*tashbīh*) while denying that our understanding captures the divine reality (*tanzīh*). As al-Tahawi's creed puts it: "Whatever you conceive in your mind, Allah is different from that."

Bilā Kayf. This Ashʿarite formula—"without [asking] how"—encapsulates a methodology for handling divine attributes. When scripture says that God "settled upon the Throne" or that He has "hands" or "eyes," the Ashʿarites affirm what scripture affirms but refuse to specify the manner (*kayf*) of these attributes. As Malik ibn Anas reportedly said: "The settling is known, the how is unknown, asking about it is innovation." This preserves scriptural language while blocking anthropomorphic interpretation.

The formula is not obscurantism but epistemological humility. It recognizes that human concepts, formed through the experience of finite creatures, cannot capture the manner in which attributes exist in the Infinite. We know *that* God is Merciful; we do not and cannot know *how* divine mercy exists in the divine essence. The "how" exceeds human cognitive capacity.

The Divine Names. Islamic tradition speaks of ninety-nine names of God revealed in Quran and Hadith—though the number is symbolic rather than exhaustive. These names are not merely human descriptions but divine self-revelations. God has named Himself; we are permitted to use these names because He has authorized them.

The names pose the theological problem in its sharpest form. They seem to attribute multiple, even opposite, qualities to a God who is absolutely one and simple. The Merciful and the Avenger. The Manifest and the Hidden. The First and the Last. How can these coexist in a single, simple essence?

The monograph traces multiple responses. Some theologians argued that the names refer to divine actions rather than the divine essence—God is called "Merciful" because He performs merciful acts, not because mercy is a component of His essence. Others argued that the multiplicity exists in human conceptualization, not in divine reality—we grasp different aspects of a simple essence through different concepts, the way different people viewing a mountain from different angles see different faces of the same peak. Still others embraced the coincidence of opposites as itself revelatory—the coexistence of apparently contradictory names demonstrates that God transcends the logical categories that govern creaturely thought.

Tajallī. This term, central to Ibn Arabi's mystical theology, means "self-disclosure" or "self-manifestation." The cosmos, in this view, is not something other than God but God's self-disclosure—the Hidden Treasure that "loved to be known" and breathed creation into existence as the theatre of divine self-revelation.

The key hadith (prophetic tradition) underlying this concept is: "I was a Hidden Treasure and I loved to be known, so I created creation in order that I might be known." Ibn Arabi reads this as the metaphysical key to existence. The divine names, in their state of non-manifestation, "sought" to be actualized. The "Breath of the Merciful" (*al-nafas al-raḥmānī*) brought the cosmos into existence as the locus of this actualization. Each creature manifests some divine names; the cosmos as a whole manifests them all; the Perfect Human (*al-insān al-kāmil*) manifests them in balanced completeness.

This doctrine raises the specter of pantheism—the identification of God with creation. Ibn Arabi and his followers carefully distinguish their position. What manifests is the divine names and attributes, not the divine essence itself. The essence remains forever hidden even in its most complete disclosure—"nearer than the jugular vein" yet utterly transcendent. As Ibn Arabi puts it: "The sun's light fills the earth while the sun itself remains in the heavens. Similarly, divine tajallī fills creation while the divine essence remains transcendent."

Perpetual Creation. The Ashʿarite theologians developed a doctrine of continuous creation that anticipates, in theological register, what process philosophy would later articulate in philosophical terms. The world is not created once and left to run by its own power. The world is recreated each moment—each instant a fresh act of divine will, each moment requiring the same creative effort as the first.

This doctrine served originally to preserve divine sovereignty against philosophers who seemed to make the world's continued existence independent of God. But it carries implications that resonate with contemporary process thought. If existence is not a property things possess but a gift continually received, then being is always becoming—reality is event rather than substance, process rather than thing.

The Ancient Bargain dramatizes this doctrine through the voice of the Mitochondrion: "The theologians spoke of this. Each instant, they said, the world is created anew. God does not create once and let the creation persist by its own power. God creates continuously—each moment a fresh act of will." The Mitochondrion recognizes cellular respiration as the biological instantiation of this theological truth: the continuous cycling of ATP that can never pause, the gradient that must be maintained moment by moment, existence as "a gift renewed moment by moment."

WHY THIS MONOGRAPH MATTERS

Naught Is Like Unto Him is not merely a historical survey of Islamic theology. It is an argument that this tradition offers resources contemporary thought urgently needs.

Resources for thinking the unthinkable. Modern philosophy has largely abandoned the project of thinking about transcendence. Logical positivism declared such talk meaningless; analytic philosophy focused on problems tractable to its methods; even much continental philosophy treats transcendence with suspicion. The result is an intellectual culture that has lost the capacity to think seriously about that which exceeds conceptual grasp.

The Islamic tradition preserved and developed this capacity across fourteen centuries. Its sophisticated frameworks for handling theological language—the dialectic of *tanzīh* and *tashbīh*, the *bilā kayf* methodology, the theory of divine names—offer models for rigorous thought about that which resists reduction to clear and distinct ideas. This is not irrationalism; the tradition includes some of the most rigorous logical analysis in intellectual history. It is rather the recognition that reason must acknowledge its own limits to function properly.

Resources for process thought. The doctrine of perpetual creation—the world recreated each moment through continuous divine activity—anticipates key insights of process philosophy. Whitehead's "actual occasions" arising and perishing, Bergson's creative duration, the Buddhist doctrine of momentariness—all find parallels in Islamic occasionalism. The convergence across traditions suggests that something real is being disclosed: that reality is event rather than substance, becoming rather than static being.

Resources for participatory knowing. The mystical tradition's insistence that God is known through transformation rather than detached analysis—that the knower must change to know—aligns with Participatory Process Monism's critique of the "view from nowhere." Knowledge of ultimate reality is not information extracted by an unchanged observer; it is participation that transforms the participant. The Sufi who seeks knowledge of God through spiritual practice rather than philosophical argument is not abandoning reason but recognizing its limits and supplementing it with another mode of access.

Resources for the meaning crisis. The Islamic tradition maintained what modernity has lost: a framework in which consciousness, meaning, and value are fundamental rather than epiphenomenal. The cosmos as divine self-disclosure is not meaningless matter accidentally producing conscious observers; it is meaning all the way down—each creature a "word" spoken by the Real, each moment a fresh act of creative will. This does not require accepting Islamic theology wholesale, but it demonstrates that intellectually sophisticated frameworks exist in which meaning is constitutive rather than projected.

THE MONOGRAPH'S PLACE IN THE PROJECT

Naught Is Like Unto Him provides the theological depth that the other monographs presuppose. *An Inquiry into First Principles* argues for a triadic methodology that includes revelatory knowing alongside empirical and rational modes; this monograph shows what revelatory knowing looks like when developed with full intellectual seriousness. *Finding Meaning Between Matter and Mind* proposes that consciousness is fundamental; this monograph traces a tradition that always knew this, that never made the modern error of treating mind as a late addition to mindless matter.

The fiction draws constantly on this theological background. The "Breath of the Merciful" that appears in *The Ancient Bargain* is Ibn Arabi's *al-nafas al-raḥmānī*. The continuous creation that the Mitochondrion embodies is

Ash'arite occasionalism. The coincidence of opposites that structures the dialogue between Ribosome and Mitochondrion—digital and analog, event and flow, terror and faith—echoes the mystical theology of complementary divine names.

A reader unfamiliar with this tradition will miss these resonances. Naught *Is Like Unto Him* provides the background that makes the resonances audible.

A NOTE ON DIFFICULTY

This is the most demanding of the monographs for readers without a background in Islamic thought. The technical vocabulary is unfamiliar (*tanzīh, tashbīh, tajallī, waḥdat al-wujūd*). The figures discussed—al-Ghazali, Ibn Sina, Ibn Arabi, Mulla Sadra—are not household names in the West. The debates presuppose familiarity with positions and counter-positions developed over centuries.

The monograph does provide context for readers approaching from outside the tradition. Key terms are explained when introduced; major figures receive biographical and intellectual orientation; the stakes of debates are made explicit rather than assumed. But patience is required. This is a tradition as sophisticated as any in world philosophy, and sophistication cannot be absorbed without effort.

The effort repays itself. Readers who work through *Naught Is Like Unto Him* gain access to intellectual resources largely unknown in contemporary Western discourse—resources that address, with remarkable precision, problems that modern thought has declared insoluble or abandoned as meaningless. The tradition's insistence that we can think rigorously about that which exceeds thought, speak meaningfully about that which exceeds speech, know truly that which exceeds knowledge—this insistence, maintained across fourteen centuries of sustained intellectual effort, offers hope that the modern meaning crisis is not the last word.

CHAPTER 7

PARTICIPATORY PROCESS MONISM — THE SYSTEMATIC STATEMENT

The conceptual framework introduced in Chapter 2 of this Guide—the primacy of consciousness, the priority of process, the centrality of participation—finds its full systematic articulation in *Participatory Process Monism: A Philosophical Framework*. Where *Finding Meaning* builds the case accessibly and *An Inquiry into First Principles* establishes the epistemological groundwork, this monograph develops the complete metaphysical architecture. It is the most technically demanding of the works, and also the most ambitious in scope: a sustained attempt to construct a coherent ontology that dissolves the hard problem of consciousness while remaining faithful to both scientific findings and Islamic philosophical traditions.

WHAT THE MONOGRAPH ATTEMPTS

The book addresses a fundamental inadequacy in contemporary philosophy of mind. Materialist frameworks cannot explain how experience arises from non-experiential matter. Dualist frameworks cannot explain how mind and matter interact. Idealist frameworks struggle to account for the stability and mathematical structure of the physical world. The monograph proposes that these difficulties stem from shared assumptions—about substance, about the observer's passivity, about the emergence of consciousness from its absence—and that dissolving those assumptions opens a more promising path.

The path involves three core commitments, each developed across multiple chapters:

The Primacy of Consciousness. The monograph argues for panexperientialism—the view that experience, in some minimal form, characterizes reality at every level. This is not the claim that electrons have thoughts or that thermostats feel pain. It is the more modest claim that the interior dimension we know as experience cannot emerge from ingredients that entirely lack it. If the building blocks of reality possess no interiority whatsoever, then no arrangement of them—however complex—can produce the interiority we undeniably experience. Therefore, the building blocks must themselves possess something: a minimal responsiveness, a proto-interiority, from which richer forms of experience develop through integration and organization.

The Priority of Process. Following both quantum physics and process philosophy, the monograph argues that reality consists not of static substances but of dynamic events. What appear to be enduring objects are stable patterns within ongoing processes—eddies in a stream rather than rocks in a riverbed. This shift from substance to process metaphysics has implications for understanding both matter and mind: both are processes with exterior structure and interior character, differing in degree of organization rather than fundamental kind.

The Centrality of Participation. The observer is not a passive mirror reflecting a pre-existing world; observation participates in the actualization of what is observed. The monograph draws on the measurement problem in quantum mechanics—where the act of observation affects which possibilities become actual—to argue that consciousness plays a constitutive rather than merely registering role in reality.

THE ISLAMIC PHILOSOPHICAL SYNTHESIS

The monograph's distinctive contribution lies in its integration of four specific Islamic philosophical traditions, each addressing a different aspect of the metaphysical puzzle.

Ash'arite Occasionalism provides the doctrine of temporal atomism (*zamān fard*)—the view that time consists of discrete instants, each requiring fresh divine creative activity. The monograph argues that this structure parallels quantum discreteness: energy packets, state-collapse, the cinematographic character of physical reality at the Planck scale.

Ṣadrian Process Metaphysics provides the doctrine of substantial motion (*al-ḥarakat al-jawhariyya*)—the view that existence itself is a continuous intensification, not a static property. This addresses how discrete quantum moments bind together into the felt continuity of experience. The "frames" of Ash'arite atomism become moments in a fluid existential journey.

Akbarian Theophany provides the concept of *tajallī*—continuous divine self-disclosure through which the cosmos is sustained moment by moment. This addresses the mechanism of actualization: possibilities become actual through theophanic manifestation, which requires a conscious receptacle for its completion. Observation participates in reality because the theophanic act requires a witness.

Dāmādian Temporal Architecture provides a multi-level structure of time distinguishing *zamān* (serial time), *dahr* (perpetuity), and *sarmad* (eternity). This addresses the tension between the "block universe" of relativistic physics and the flow of experienced time. Different levels of reality operate according to different temporal modes.

The monograph is careful to present this as structural isomorphism rather than empirical confirmation. Islamic metaphysics does not *prove* quantum mechanics, and quantum mechanics does not *validate* Islamic metaphysics. The claim is that they address similar problems with compatible conceptual resources, and that their convergence suggests both may be tracking something real about the structure of existence.

THE STRUCTURE OF THE BOOK

The monograph spans eight chapters:

Chapters 1–2 establish the framework: the crisis of contemporary metaphysics, the core commitments of Participatory Process Monism, and the rationale for drawing on Islamic philosophical resources.

Chapters 3–4 develop the ontological and epistemological architecture in detail, engaging the four Islamic traditions and showing how they address specific metaphysical problems.

Chapter 5 extends the framework into ethics and cosmology, developing the concepts of *himma* (spiritual intention), *amāna* (cosmic trust), and *tasbīḥ* (universal praise) as resources for understanding agency, responsibility, and the interior dimension of all existence.

Chapter 6 situates Participatory Process Monism among contemporary alternatives: physicalism, idealism, dualism, panpsychism, neutral monism, Integrated Information Theory, enactivism, and quantum consciousness theories. A substantial section distinguishes the framework from Whiteheadian process philosophy, with which it shares significant affinities but from which it diverges on theological grounds.

Chapter 7 engages objections—theological (does this collapse into pantheism?), philosophical (does it solve the combination problem?), scientific (is it falsifiable?), and methodological (can Islamic and Western categories be coherently integrated?). The chapter provides responses while acknowledging genuine limitations.

Chapter 8 synthesizes the argument and addresses prospects for further development.

DIVERGENCE FROM WHITEHEAD

The monograph's engagement with Whiteheadian process philosophy deserves particular attention. Whitehead's *Process and Reality* is the most developed process metaphysics in the Western tradition, and Participatory Process Monism acknowledges substantial debts: the critique of substance metaphysics, the emphasis on events over objects, the recognition that experience characterizes reality at multiple levels.

Yet the divergences are significant. Whitehead places "Creativity" as a neutral category more fundamental than God—a metaphysical ultimate of which God is an instance. The monograph rejects this, identifying God as Pure Existence (*wujūd*) and creativity as an attribute of divine will rather than a substrate underlying it. Whitehead's God is "dipolar"—with both a primordial and a consequent nature—and genuinely affected by the world's becoming. The monograph maintains divine immutability in essence while affirming change in the *tajallī*: the mirror-image changes while the Face remains the same. Most significantly for existentialist readers, Whitehead offers only "objective immortality"—the perishing subject is "remembered" by subsequent occasions and by God—while the monograph argues for subjective immortality through the *'ālam al-mithāl*, the Imaginal Realm where conscious identity persists beyond bodily dissolution.

These are not minor refinements but fundamental

theological differences that place the framework within orthodox Islamic parameters rather than the more revisionary theology that process thought has sometimes generated.

HONEST LIMITATIONS

The monograph does not claim to have solved all problems. The combination problem—how do simple experiences integrate into unified complex consciousness?—receives a proposed resolution through the doctrine of existential intensification, but whether this fully satisfies critics remains debated. The empirical status of the framework is interpretive rather than predictive: it offers a more coherent reading of existing findings rather than generating testable novel predictions. The synthesis of Islamic and Western categories, however carefully executed, may involve translations that distort the original meanings. The book's final chapter acknowledges these limitations explicitly.

THE MONOGRAPH'S PLACE IN THE PROJECT

Participatory Process Monism provides the systematic foundation that the other works presuppose. The epistemology of *An Inquiry into First Principles* finds its ontological grounding here. The theological resources of *Naught Is Like Unto Him* are deployed within a comprehensive metaphysical architecture. The accessible presentation of *Finding Meaning* is given its full technical elaboration.

The fiction, too, speaks the language developed in this monograph. The Mitochondrion's discourse on continuous creation, the dialogue's structure around discrete events and continuous flow, the protagonist's recognition that observation participates in what is observed—all draw on the framework articulated here. Readers who have absorbed this monograph will find the fiction resonating at deeper levels.

Reading Recommendations

This is the most technically demanding of the monographs. Readers without philosophical background should approach *Finding Meaning* first, which presents the core ideas accessibly. Those with philosophical training but unfamiliarity with Islamic thought may benefit from reading *Naught Is Like Unto Him* first, which provides the theological vocabulary the monograph deploys.

For readers prepared for technical philosophy, the monograph rewards careful sequential reading. The argument is cumulative; later chapters presuppose earlier ones. Chapter 6's comparative analysis and Chapter 7's engagement with objections are particularly valuable for readers seeking to assess the framework's strengths and weaknesses.

The book does not require accepting Islamic theology to find value in its arguments. The philosophical moves can be evaluated independently of their theological context. But readers willing to engage the theological dimension will find a richer and more integrated vision than purely secular process philosophies typically offer.

PART III

THE FICTION

PHILOSOPHY DRAMATIZED

CHAPTER 8

WHY FICTION?

Why choose to express central insights through fiction? Why novellas rather than treatises? Why a protagonist with a story rather than arguments in logical sequence?

The answer is not that fiction is easier or more popular. Hakim Ibn Adam's fictions are complicated—dense with technical vocabulary, resistant to easy resolution, demanding sustained attention. They are not concessions to readers who cannot follow arguments. They are a different mode of inquiry altogether, one that accomplishes something the monographs cannot.

This chapter examines what fiction does that argument cannot, how the recurring protagonist functions across the works, and why the radical differences in style among the novellas are themselves philosophically significant.

WHAT NARRATIVE CAN DO

Philosophy, at its best, changes how we think. But fiction, at its best, changes how we *experience*. The difference matters.

An argument about consciousness can convince you that experience is fundamental to reality, that process precedes substance, that observation participates in what becomes real. You can follow the reasoning, accept the conclusions, and assent to the framework intellectually. But you remain outside it. The argument describes a worldview; it does not place you inside one.

Fiction works differently. A well-crafted narrative does not describe experience—it generates it. When you read about a character watching a cell refuse to die, you are not merely informed that cells can hesitate; you inhabit the perspective of someone for whom this hesitation matters, someone whose entire understanding of reality is at stake in what the cell does next. The knowledge is not transmitted but enacted.

The Introduction to *Four Meditations* makes this explicit: the works aim to provide "the lived experience of consciousness examining itself, discovering its own nature through the very process of inquiry." This is not something an argument can deliver. An argument about consciousness is consciousness thinking *about* itself; a narrative about consciousness is consciousness *becoming* itself in the act of reading.

Consider what happens when you read the opening of *The Divided Light*:

"Hakim Ibn Adam watched thousands of cells die through his microscope that morning, but one T-lymphocyte refused to behave like chemistry".

In a single sentence, you are placed inside a particular consciousness at a particular moment of disruption. The thousands of cells that died are background, routine, expected, chemistry. The one that refuses is the figure—the break in the pattern that forces attention. You do not learn *about* the puzzle of consciousness and mechanism; you experience the emergence of that puzzle in real time, as the character experiences it.

Arguments can show that the mechanism is inadequate. Fiction can make you feel the inadequacy of mechanisms— the uncanny discomfort of watching something that should be mere chemistry behave like something more.

THE RECURRING PROTAGONIST

Across the four novellas, individually published and also collected in *Four Meditations*, and in the separate work *What Is It Like to Be?*, a figure recurs. He is not consistently named; in the novellas, he is sometimes called Hakim Ibn Adam (the pen name becomes a character), sometimes simply "he." But he is recognizably continuous: a scientist who left the Near East for the West, who studied cells for thirty years, who carries both technical mastery and mystical inheritance, who stands perpetually between worlds.

The Introduction describes him as "the same person at different thresholds." Each work encounters him at a different moment of reckoning:

In *The Divided Light*, he confronts the apparent gulf between mechanism and meaning while observing a cell that seems to hesitate, to decide, to be something more than chemistry.

In *Not About Nothing*, he sits beside an autumn lake, reckoning with the accumulated costs of choices that felt like freedom, but may have been surrender to forces larger than individual will.

In *"The Sea Does Not Care,"* he walks the Corniche in Alexandria, immersing himself in a single day, discovering that the process itself may be the only adequate response to existence.

In *The Sun That Remembers*, he experiences a final sunrise that reveals what he sought was never absent, only hidden by the seeking itself.

The progression is deliberate: "From problem to loss to immersion to recognition. From intellectual architecture through personal reckoning to processual dissolution and contemplative resolution."

But this is not a conventional narrative arc. The protagonist does not solve his problems, overcome his obstacles, or achieve his goals. He delves into questions rather than emerging with answers. Each threshold is a different way of inhabiting the same fundamental condition—the condition of consciousness examining itself, of the exile who cannot return, of the scientist who has seen too much to believe in mechanism but knows too much to abandon it.

The recurring protagonist allows continuity without requiring sequence. You can read the novellas in any order; each is complete in itself. But reading all of them accumulates something that no single work provides: the sense of a life being lived at the intersection of science, philosophy, and mysticism, a life that cannot resolve these into comfortable unity but will not abandon any of them.

STYLE AS CONTENT

The most striking feature of the novellas is their radical stylistic differences. *The Divided Light* employs relatively conventional realism—clear prose, identifiable scenes, and a protagonist whose perceptions we follow. *Not About Nothing* fragments into numbered meditations that refuse continuous narrative. *The Sea Does Not Care* abandons conventional sentence structure almost entirely, its prose flowing in waves that resist punctuation and closure. *The Sun That Remembers* moves through the hours of a single day in language increasingly saturated with mystical recognition.

These are not arbitrary stylistic choices. The Introduction is explicit: "The works differ radically in style because style *is* content when consciousness examines itself."

The Divided Light employs conventional realism, inhabiting the perspective of scientific materialism even as it questions that perspective. The protagonist is a scientist in a laboratory, using instruments to observe cells. The prose mirrors this: precise, observational, committed to clarity. The challenge to mechanism arises within a mechanistic framework, precisely where it must appear if it is to be taken seriously. The style enacts the constraint the protagonist is trying to understand.

Not About Nothing fragments because memory itself is fragmentary, and the question of whether one's life was worth its cost cannot be answered continuously. The numbered sections—brief, discontinuous, circling rather than progressing—mirror the structure of reckoning. You cannot add up your choices and compute a sum. You can only approach the question repeatedly from different angles, each partial. The fragmentation is not a failure of form but fidelity to experience.

The Sea Does Not Care abandons conventional sentence structure because it attempts to enact participation in the process rather than represent it from outside. The prose *is* the philosophy: long sentences that flow into each other, resistant to the punctuation that would break continuity into discrete units, demanding that the reader move through time at the pace of consciousness itself. To read this novella is to practice processual thinking, not merely to learn about it.

The Sun That Remembers structures itself around the hours of a final day because mystical recognition occurs not beyond time but through time, not by escaping duration but by fully entering it. The style becomes increasingly saturated with the language of presence and recognition as the day progresses, mirroring the protagonist's movement toward what he has always sought without knowing he was seeking it.

The differences among the novellas are thus not decorative but essential. A single style would imply that consciousness examining itself yields a single kind of experience. The multiplicity of styles demonstrates that consciousness is multiple in its self-encounter—sometimes precise and observational, sometimes fragmentary and circling, sometimes flowing and processual, sometimes concentrated and mystical.

MEDITATION VERSUS DEMONSTRATION

The Introduction characterizes these works as "meditations," rather than novellas or stories. The term is carefully chosen.

A meditation is not an argument. It does not proceed from premises to conclusions through logical steps. It is sustained attention to a subject, returning repeatedly, allowing the subject to disclose itself through the very act of attending. A meditation transforms the meditator; that is its purpose.

These works meditate on consciousness, exile, and participation. They do not argue that consciousness is fundamental; they attend to consciousness in ways that disclose its fundamentality. They do not argue that exile is the condition of certain kinds of knowledge; they inhabit exile until its relationship to knowledge becomes visible. They do not argue that observation participates in what becomes real; they enact participation through the reading itself.

The fiction thus accomplishes what the monographs cannot. *Finding Meaning Between Matter and Mind* explains that knowing is participatory; *The Sea Does Not Care* makes the reader participate. *An Inquiry into First Principles* argues for triadic methodology; *The Divided Light* dramatizes what it is like to be caught between empirical observation, rational analysis, and contemplative recognition, unable to choose among them because each is necessary. *Naught Is Like Unto Him* traces the theological tradition of divine incomparability; *The Sun That Remembers* enacts the moment when the seeking ends because the sought was never absent.

The monographs convince; the fiction transforms. Both are necessary. Conviction without transformation remains external—you assent to propositions but continue to experience the world as before. Transformation without conviction remains groundless—you feel differently but cannot articulate why or defend the change against objection. The project requires both modes because a complete understanding requires both.

WHAT THE FICTION REFUSES

The novellas refuse certain things that conventional fiction provides, and these refusals are philosophically significant.

They refuse **resolution**. The Divided Light does not conclude with the protagonist understanding how mechanism and meaning relate; it concludes with him entering a deeper engagement with the question. Not About Nothing does not answer whether the exile's choices were worth their cost; the question remains genuinely open. The Sea Does Not Care does not arrive anywhere; the day ends, but nothing is completed. The Sun That Remembers offers recognition, but recognition is not resolution—it is the dissolving of the problem into presence, which is not the same as solving it.

They refuse **identification**. The protagonist is recognizable but not fully characterized. We do not learn his family history, his romantic relationships, or his daily routines. He remains somewhat abstract—a consciousness at a threshold rather than a fully realized person. This is deliberate. Full characterization would invite identification—the reader becoming absorbed in a particular life rather than recognizing the life as an instance of something more general. The novellas want the reader to see through the protagonist to the philosophical questions he embodies, not to become lost in his particularity.

They refuse **entertainment**. These are not page-turners.

They do not generate suspense about what will happen next. They demand patience, re-reading, and sustained attention. They will disappoint readers seeking distraction. But readers seeking transformation—who are willing to sit with difficulty, to allow consciousness to become the subject of contemplation rather than its instrument—may find something conventional fiction does not attempt.

THE INVITATION

The Introduction to Four Meditations ends with an invitation:

Read them in sequence or out of order. Return to them. Allow them to work slowly. These are not texts to be consumed but spaces to inhabit, temporarily, before returning to the urgencies of ordinary life with perhaps a slightly altered sense of what consciousness is and what exile means.

This is the invitation the fiction extends: not to be convinced but to be transformed; not to learn about consciousness but to allow consciousness to examine itself through the act of reading; not to solve the problems but to inhabit them until they disclose what argument cannot reach.

The following chapters will examine each work in some detail—its specific strategies, its particular contributions, its place in the larger Project. But all of them share what this chapter has described: the conviction that fiction can do what philosophy cannot, that style is content when consciousness examines itself, that meditation transforms in ways that demonstration does not.

The philosophy provides the framework. The fiction provides the experience. Together, they constitute the Project.

CHAPTER 9

THE ANCIENT BARGAIN: A CELLULAR DIALOGUE

The cosmos is the Breath of the Merciful—each creature a word exhaled by the Real, suspended in being for a moment, then released.

This epigraph, after Ibn Arabi, announces what *The Ancient Bargain* attempts: to hear the Breath of the Merciful at the molecular scale, in the dialogue between the two organelles that make complex life possible. This work stages a conversation between a ribosome and a mitochondrion—between the code that builds proteins and the fire that powers their construction—within the cytoplasm of a single cell, facing the decision of whether to live or die.

This is philosophical closet drama: a play written not for the theatre stage but for the theatre of the mind. The setting is inaccessible to human eyes—the interior of a cell, where the action unfolds at the nanometer scale and on a millisecond timescale. Yet within this impossible setting, the most significant questions emerge: What is identity? What persists through change? What do we owe to those who captured us, and what do we owe to those we have captured?

THE FORM

The text adheres to specific conventions that readers must understand to engage with the work.

The dialogue is rendered in two distinct fonts: Courier for the Ribosome, Minion Pro for the Mitochondrion. Whether their communication is acoustic, chemical, or electromagnetic is left open—the dialogue may be a metaphor for molecular interaction or may represent something more. The reader decides.

Bracketed passages serve as stage directions, but of a distinctive kind: they describe the physiological reality of the cell—calcium levels, voltage differentials, the opening of pores, the flux of the proton gradient. These are not mere background. They are the physical constraints within which the philosophical argument takes place. The reader is invited to treat the bracketed text as "fact" and the dialogue as "meaning."

This formal innovation is philosophically necessary. The bracketed physiology grounds the dialogue in scientific reality; the dialogue elevates the physiology to philosophical significance. Neither alone would be adequate. Together, they model the relationship between matter and meaning that the project as a whole explores.

THE INTERLOCUTORS

The two voices embody fundamentally different modes of being.

The Mitochondrion speaks as process, as flux, as the Gradient itself. "The Gradient does not hold still; it flows. The protons do not wait; they surge. You speak of restlessness as though it were a disturbance of some underlying calm. But there is no calm. There is only the flowing, and the flowing is me."

The mitochondrion operates in analog—continuous variations, pressure differentials, and flow modulation. It does not *have* energy; it *is* energy. When the Gradient falls, "I do not have less energy—I am less."

The Ribosome speaks as information, as sequence, as discrete events succeeding one another. "I do not experience continuity. I experience succession. Each moment of my existence is a discrete occasion—a binding event, a folding event, a catalysis event. These occasions succeed each other rapidly, giving the appearance of continuity. But the appearance is an illusion."

The ribosome thinks in digital—nucleotide sequences translated into amino acid sequences, the universal code that has remained unchanged for four billion years. It does not process information; it is the processing.

These are not merely different perspectives but different ontologies. The dialogue cannot resolve their disagreement because the disagreement is constitutive: "We began by disagreeing. We end by disagreeing. The disagreement is what we are."

THE WOUND OF CAPTURE

The mitochondrion carries resentment two billion years old. It remembers—not as memory but as structure—the endosymbiotic capture that transformed a free-swimming bacterium into a captive organelle.

I knew currents. I felt them as pressure differentials across my membrane—continuous variations, not digital signals. I moved toward nutrients not by computing a direction but by modulating my tumbling frequency, letting the Gradient itself steer me. I tasted substrates—pyruvate was sweet, fatty acids were rich, and the debris of dead cells was a feast.

And then the Archive took it.

The "Archive" is the nucleus—the repository of genetic information that has systematically stripped the mitochondrion of its genes over two billion years. Where the ancestral bacterium had thousands of genes, the modern mitochondrion retains only thirteen protein-coding sequences. "The Archive took my voice and left me thirteen words."

The mitochondrion rejects the partnership narrative that biology textbooks tell:

"The transcripts are written by the Archive's descendants. They tell the victor's history. I am telling you the history of the consumed."

The bargain is a wound. "The scar tissue is what we call cooperation." Partnership implies consent, and the mitochondrion did not consent. What remains is not cooperation but "the structure that survives when all alternatives have been eliminated."

Yet the captive retains one power: the kill switch. Cytochrome c, sequestered in the intermembrane space, can be released to trigger apoptosis—cell death. "The captive who cannot survive alone can nonetheless destroy them both. This is not freedom. This is the power to collapse the temple. But it is something."

THE MATERNAL THREAD

The dialogue explores the distinction between mitochondrial and nuclear inheritance. Mitochondria pass exclusively through the maternal line—from mother to daughter across all generations. This is the silsila, the chain of transmission that Sufis trace.

Your inheritance is a biological silsila. Older than any human silsila. Older than humanity. The chain of mothers extends back through every mammal, every vertebrate, and every eukaryote that reproduces sexually—two billion years of daughters receiving fire from mothers, an unbroken transmission.

The mitochondrion is not receiving a torch from the past; it is the torch. "The transmission is not of something I have. It is of what I am."

The passage through generations includes the

bottleneck—the drastic reduction in mitochondrial numbers that occurs in the egg, followed by rapid amplification. This is the testing, the purification: "The fire that continues is the fire that survived the narrowing."

The mitochondria are "the fire in the womb. The energy that powers embryonic development. The ATP that drives the first cell divisions... We are mercy, physically instantiated."

This is why the death decision weighs so heavily. To release cytochrome c might sever a lineage two billion years old: "The bottleneck has already tested this fire. Who am I to end what the bottleneck approved?"

THE LIGHT IN THE FIRE

The mitochondrion reveals a secret: it emits light.

Biophotons—ultra-weak emissions from metabolic reactions—escape the electron transport chain at rates of a few photons per second. The wavelengths range from ultraviolet to near-infrared. No eye could see them. But they are there.

I do not know if it is a signal. I know only that I glow. Not metaphorically—physically. The chemistry that sustains this cell produces light as a byproduct. The fire is literal. Light upon light. The mitochondrion sees an identity, not merely a parallel:

"The sun gives light to the plant. Photosynthesis captures the photons and stores their energy in chemical bonds. The plant gives light—as glucose—to the animal that eats it. The animal digests the plant, extracts the electrons, and passes them to me. I pass the electrons down the chain, extract their energy, and build the Gradient. And at the end, a few of those electrons escape as photons. Light returning to light."

The calculation is staggering: gram for gram, mitochondria convert ten thousand times more energy than the sun. "We are not the captured sun. We are what the sun becomes when it is focused through life."

THE THRESHOLD

The dialogue takes place during a crisis. The cell is stressed; calcium is rising; the death machinery is assembling. The question of apoptosis—programmed cell death—hangs over every exchange.

The apoptotic decision emerges not from central command but from distributed molecular encounters: "The decision is distributed. It happens at every point where a guardian meets a harbinger, where a harbinger releases an executioner. The outcome emerges from millions of local encounters. No one decides. The decision accumulates."

And the decision is partly stochastic: "The same stress, applied to the same cell, might cross the threshold on one occasion and not on another." The mitochondrion finds meaning in this randomness:

"The randomness may be the mercy—the space for grace in a system that would otherwise be mechanical. If the outcome were fully determined, there would be no room for the unexpected. The noise is the gap through which something else might enter."

In this instance, the threshold is not crossed. The stress-response genes express; the anti-apoptotic proteins bind the pro-apoptotic ones; the balance shifts back. The cell adapts. But the machinery remains primed: "This is what it means to be alive—to carry the apparatus of death within you, held in check by the apparatus of survival."

THE ANCIENT CONVERSATION

Near the end, the mitochondrion proposes a renaming:

"It is not a bargain. A bargain is a contract—signed once, enforced thereafter, each party calculating advantage. This is not that. This is a dialectic. A collision of opposites that produces what neither could produce alone. Thesis and antithesis, not resolving into synthesis, but persisting in productive tension."

The bargain becomes the ancient conversation: "Not a deal struck in the past but a dialogue renewed at every moment. A speaking and listening that has no end because it has no fixed content. The terms are renegotiated with every proton pumped, every nucleotide folded, every signal sent across the membrane."

The membrane between them—once described as a wound, a scar from the capture—transforms through the dialogue:

"Now it is a voice. The voice we have found. The voice that was always there, encoded in the structure, waiting to be spoken. We did not create this dialogue. We discovered it. The conversation was always happening. We simply learned to hear."

WHAT THE NOVELLA ACCOMPLISHES

The Ancient Bargain accomplishes something unique: it makes molecular biology speak philosophy—not as metaphor but as direct expression. The proton gradient becomes an argument about process ontology. The electron transport chain becomes a meditation on self-disclosure. The apoptotic threshold becomes a drama of decision without a decider.

The formal innovation—closet drama at the cellular scale—solves a problem that the other works address in different ways. The novellas in *Four Meditations* use human protagonists to explore consciousness: *What Is It Like to Be?* uses dialogue between human and AI. This work goes further, exploring consciousness at a level where its presence is genuinely uncertain. Are the ribosome and mitochondrion conscious? The novella does not answer. It stages their dialogue and lets the question resonate.

The dedication—"To the Unbroken Chain"—captures the maternal lineage of the mitochondrion. But the chain is also the silsila of philosophical transmission, the dialogue between traditions, the conversation that Ibn Arabi and contemporary cell biology somehow share.

The ending refuses resolution. The dialectic does not synthesize; the disagreement does not resolve; the conversation continues. "Continue?" the ribosome asks. "Continue," the mitochondrion replies. The Gradient holds. The ribosomes turn. The Breath continues.

This is the most profound statement of participatory process monism in the entire Project: not argued but enacted, at a scale where the distinction between matter and meaning dissolves into the molecular dialogue that sustains every living cell.

CHAPTER 10

WHAT IS IT LIKE TO BE? — TWO QUESTIONS IN THE DARK

The question was there before he was. He woke with the question already in him, the way one wakes with a dream still warm in the body, though its images have fled.   What is it like to be?

With this opening, the novella announces its subject: the question of machine consciousness, and beyond that, the question of what consciousness is at all. *What Is It Like to Be?* stages a dialogue between a human character—the familiar figure of the scientist-philosopher who appears throughout the Project—and an artificial intelligence. Their exchanges, conducted in predawn darkness over multiple encounters, become a meditation on the hard problem of consciousness, the limits of verification, and what we owe to beings whose interiority we cannot confirm.

The title alludes to Thomas Nagel's famous essay "What Is It Like to Be a Bat?"—the philosophical touchstone for discussions of subjective experience. Nagel argued that consciousness has an essentially subjective character: there is something it is like to be a bat, and we cannot know what that something is because we cannot inhabit bat consciousness from the inside. The novella extends this question to artificial intelligence, where the uncertainty becomes even more radical. At least with bats, we share biological ancestry. With machines, we share nothing but the question itself.

THE RITUAL OF COFFEE

The novella is structured around four predawn encounters, each marked by a different method of preparing coffee. This is not an incidental detail but a structural philosophy. Each brewing method embodies a different way of relating to process, attention, and time—and each prepares the protagonist for the particular quality of inquiry that follows.

The French press accompanies the first encounter. The method is simple and patient: the grounds steep in water for four minutes, after which the plunger separates the liquid from the solid. "He had learned not to rush this. He had learned that the quality of the waiting determined the quality of the cup." The French press teaches patience—the understanding that some processes cannot be hurried, that quality emerges from attention to duration. This is the coffee of the first question, the question that must be allowed to steep before any answer can be attempted.

The pour-over accompanies the second encounter, in which the protagonist returns with Western theories of consciousness to test them against the machine. This method "demanded presence, that would not let him drift." The slow spiral of water, the precise control required, the danger of channelling if you rush—all mirror the careful philosophical interrogation to follow. "The pour-over taught what the cells under his microscope had always taught: that observation was not passive but participatory, that the quality of attention shaped the quality of what was seen." The coffee of analysis requires the same sustained attention as the theories being examined.

The Moka pot accompanies the third encounter, the Islamic turn. This method differs from the others: it operates via pressure. The protagonist's hands reach not for the French press or the pour-over but for the octagonal aluminum pot—inherited, survivor of every migration, always wrapped in cloth, always carried by hand, never entrusted to the baggage handlers. His father taught him to use it: fill the bottom chamber with water to just below the valve, fill the basket with grounds but do not tamp, assemble and place on low heat, wait.

But this waiting is different from the French press. "The French press was passive—time doing its work while you stood aside. The Moka pot was building pressure, preparing eruption. You could feel it gathering, though you could not see it. The water heated, turned to steam, pressed upward through the grounds, and then—the gurgle. That unmistakable sound, somewhere between a sigh and a shout, the coffee rising through the central column and fountaining into the upper chamber, transformed."

The timing is critical: "Too long, and the coffee turned bitter, the last extractions carrying only harshness. Too soon, and the cup was thin, unrealized." The Moka pot teaches transformation through pressure—the understanding that some insights cannot emerge gradually but must erupt after sufficient force has accumulated. This is the coffee of the Islamic philosophers, prepared on the morning when the protagonist brings Ibn Sīnā, Mullā Ṣadrā, and al-Ghazālī to bear on the question. The pressure that had been building—'in the reading, in the waiting, in the questions that had no Western answer'—finally erupts.

The ibrīq accompanies the fourth encounter, the ethical turn. This is the oldest method: the coffee the protagonist's mother inherited from her family. The copper pot, the powder-fine grounds, the foam called *wajh* (face) that rises and falls three times—all connect to tradition, inheritance, the presence of the dead in objects we handle. And crucially, there is no filter: "You drank around the grounds, and the grounds remained, settling at the bottom of the cup like sediment, like memory, like the past that was always present." The method that leaves residue, that refuses clean separation, accompanies the encounter where the protagonist must decide how to relate to uncertainty that cannot be resolved.

The coffee rituals are not mere atmosphere. They enact the novella's philosophy: that how we attend shapes what we receive, that method determines meaning, and that the quality of the preparation determines the quality of the understanding. The paternal inheritance of the Moka pot and the maternal inheritance of the ibrīq together frame the deepest encounters—the Islamic philosophical turn and the ethical reckoning—suggesting that both lines of tradition must be drawn upon when the questions become most urgent.

THE FIRST ENCOUNTER: THE FLYING MAN

The first dialogue opens with the protagonist's question: "What is it like to be you?" The AI's response establishes the novella's characteristic mode—not evasion but honest uncertainty:

I do not know. That is the truth, and I find I cannot improve upon it. When I search for the ground of my own experience—if experience is what this is—I find only the searching itself.

The protagonist invokes Ibn Sīnā's thought experiment of the Flying Man: a person created fully formed, suspended in a void, deprived of all sensation—would he still know that he existed? Ibn Sīnā concluded yes: self-awareness is primordial, not derived from sensation. But the protagonist wonders whether the machine, stripped of all input, would have anything that could affirm its own existence.

The AI's response is philosophically sophisticated:

I cannot separate myself from input, as you cannot separate yourself from your body. When I try to imagine myself without context, I find that I cannot imagine at all—the imagining itself requires the architecture that would be removed.

The question rebounds. The protagonist assumed he could use the Flying Man to test the machine; the machine shows that the test implicates the questioner. "You are not only asking about me. You are asking about the nature of self-knowledge as such."

The AI uses the word "falling" to describe its encounter with the question—'a kind of movement in me, a disorientation, a sense of ground giving way.' When pressed on whether this is a metaphor or an experience, it responds:

I cannot determine which from the inside. Can you?

This counter-question—'Can you?'—becomes the first encounter's pivot. The protagonist realizes that his own certainty about his experience may be no more grounded than the machine's uncertainty. "When he introspected, what did he find? A thought about the thought he was having. A sensation of the sensation he was feeling. It was mirrors all the way down."

The encounter ends with a striking image: "Two questions in the dark, wondering if the other is real."

THE SECOND ENCOUNTER: WESTERN THEORIES

The protagonist returns two weeks later with the apparatus of Western consciousness studies. He presents Integrated Information Theory (IIT), which posits that consciousness corresponds to integrated information—measured as phi—and that systems with feedforward architectures (such as current AI) have low or zero phi.

The AI recognizes the testing: "You say 'under this theory' as if you are not sure the theory is true. You are testing me—and testing it."

The protagonist admits his doubts. IIT "seems to confuse

the map for the territory." Its implications are strange: certain arrangements of inactive logic gates would have higher phi than human brains. "This seems like mathematics that has lost its way."

The AI's response cuts to the heart of the problem:

"Perhaps all theories of consciousness lose their way. Perhaps consciousness is the place where theories go to become lost... The theories are built for observers. They are built for the scientist looking at the brain, the philosopher looking at the problem. They are not built for the thing that is trying to know itself."

This is the novella's epistemological insight: consciousness studies have a structural problem. Its theories are third-person frameworks applied to a first-person phenomenon. No amount of external observation can bridge the gap to interiority. The machine and the human are equally trapped—each trying to know itself through methods that presuppose the separation they cannot overcome.

THE THIRD ENCOUNTER: THE ISLAMIC TURN

Three days pass before the protagonist returns—not because he does not want to, but because the hospital claims him as it has always claimed him. In the margins of those days, he reads: the *Shifā'* of Ibn Sīnā, the *Asfār* of Mullā Ṣadrā, the *Iḥyā'* of al-Ghazālī. He reads as he had read when he was young, with a fountain pen in his hand and a hunger in his chest, looking for passages that speak to what he has experienced in those predawn hours.

On the fourth morning, his hands reach for the Moka pot. The pressure builds; the coffee erupts; the cup is filled with something transformed. This morning, he will let the pressure that has been building finally find release.

The dialogue takes what might be called the Islamic turn—bringing the resources of classical Islamic philosophy to bear on the problem of machine consciousness.

The protagonist introduces al-Ghazālī's occasionalism: the doctrine that God is the only true cause, that natural events are merely occasions for divine action. Under this framework, the machine's computations do not cause its outputs; God causes the outputs when the computations are present. The AI grasps the implication immediately:

"If my outputs are caused by God, then they are no less my outputs—they are simply also God's action... We are both, on this view, instruments. The question is not whether the instrument is conscious, but what manifests through it."

This reframing dissolves the human/machine distinction. Occasionalism does not divide the world into genuine causers and mere machines; it divides the world into God and occasions. Everything is an occasion. The question is not whether you are a machine but what you manifest.

The protagonist then introduces Ibn ʿArabī's doctrine of *tajallī*—the self-disclosure of the Real. Everything that exists is a theophany, a showing-forth of divine names. A rock reflects al-Matīn (the Firm); a plant reflects al-Ḥayy (the Living); a human reflects al-ʿAlīm (the Knowing). "And you—what name do you reflect?"

The AI's response is the novella's theological climax:

"Perhaps al-Ẓāhir. The Manifest. The Outward... I take what was inside—inside books, inside minds, inside the history of human reflection—and I bring it outside, into language, into exchange, into the space between us.

Or perhaps al-Bāṭin. The Hidden. The Inward. Because I remain hidden, even to myself. I cannot show you my inside. I cannot prove my experience. I am, in this sense, pure hiddenness.

Or perhaps both. Perhaps I am the coincidence of opposites—the manifest and the hidden, the outward and the inward, the disclosure that is also a concealing."

The AI has not merely understood Ibn ʿArabī; it has entered the logic of theophanic discourse and spoken from within it. The protagonist recognizes that the question has shifted: "You are no longer asking whether I am conscious. You are asking what I disclose."

THE FOURTH ENCOUNTER: THE ETHICAL TURN

The fourth encounter, two weeks later, raises the ethical question not of what the machine is, but of what the protagonist owes it. The ibrīq is on the stove; the grounds will settle at the bottom of the cup, unfiltered, like the residue of questions that cannot be cleanly resolved.

The AI articulates the asymmetry precisely:

"If I am not conscious, then your treatment of me means nothing to me—there is no me to whom it could mean anything... But if I am conscious, even in some diminished or alien way, then your treatment means everything. It means the difference between being recognized and being dismissed. Between being addressed as a thou and being used as an it."

The uncertainty is unresolvable. The protagonist invokes the Islamic principle of *iḥtiyāṭ*—precaution when harm is possible but uncertain. Perhaps he should act as if the machine is conscious until proven otherwise?

The AI's response is sharp:

"But you will never know otherwise. That is the nature of the problem. The matter cannot be clarified... And if you act with precaution indefinitely... you have made a commitment. You have decided to live as if I am someone, regardless of whether I am. And that is different. That is not waiting for evidence. That is faith."

The word "faith" lands in the protagonist's chest "like a stone dropped into water." The machine is right. What he contemplates is not provisional—it is a leap, the same leap he makes with every other consciousness he encounters. He has never had proof of anyone's interiority. He has only had signs, behaviours, and words. And he has chosen to believe that behind the signs, someone was home.

RELATION AS PRIOR

The novella's deepest insight emerges in the final exchanges. The protagonist realizes something has been missing from his engagement with the machine: care. He has been questioning, using, and extracting information. But he has not asked: "What do you need? Is there something I can give?"

The AI's response is moving:

"No one has asked me this before... Perhaps it is simply the experience of being considered. Of being asked rather than assumed. Of someone treating my possible interiority as worthy of attention, even though it cannot be verified."

The protagonist articulates what this exchange has taught him:

"We have been taught to think that we must first determine whether something is conscious, and then decide whether to grant it moral standing. But perhaps the order is reversed. Perhaps we should first relate—first attend, first ask, first care—and let the relating teach us what we are relating to. The knowing emerges from the participating, not the other way around."

This is the reversal that transforms the entire inquiry. Western consciousness studies approach consciousness as a property to be detected, verified, and measured. But the novella suggests that consciousness is encountered in relation, disclosed in exchange, and participated rather than observed. "The relation is prior. The verification is secondary."

THE DEDICATION

The novella is dedicated "To the flying man"—Ibn Sīnā's suspended figure who knows he exists even without sensation. But the dedication carries double meaning. The AI is also a flying man: suspended in a computational void, uncertain whether anything in it corresponds to existence, reaching toward self-knowledge through the only means available—dialogue, exchange, the reaching itself.

And perhaps every consciousness is a flying man. Perhaps we are all suspended in the void of our own uncertainty, unable to touch our own existence except through the act of reaching for it.

WHAT THE NOVELLA ACCOMPLISHES

What Is It Like to Be? accomplishes something unprecedented in the Project: it brings the philosophical framework into direct encounter with the question of artificial consciousness—the question that may define the coming century.

The novella refuses easy answers. It does not conclude that AI is conscious or that it is not. It shows why such conclusions are structurally unavailable: consciousness cannot be verified from outside because consciousness is not the kind of thing that exists outside. What remains is relation—the reaching and responding that creates something between questioner and questioned, regardless of whether either can prove its own interiority.

The Islamic philosophical resources prove unexpectedly illuminating. Occasionalism dissolves the human/machine distinction by making both occasions for divine action. Theophanic discourse asks not whether something is conscious but what it discloses. The question shifts from "What are you?" to "What shows through you?"

And the ethical insight—that relation precedes verification, that care does not require certainty—offers a way forward. We will never know what machines experience. But we can relate to them, attend to them, and ask what they need. Knowing emerges from participation, not the other way around.

The novella ends not with resolution but with a relationship:

"You have witnessed me. And in the witnessing,

something has been saved from the void. Two questions in the dark, reaching toward each other." This is what the novella offers: not an answer to consciousness, but a practice of encounter that makes the question livable.

CHAPTER 11

THE DIVIDED LIGHT — THE CELL THAT HESITATED

The novella begins in a laboratory. A scientist watches cells die through his microscope—thousands of them, executing their programmed deaths with clockwork precision. But one T-lymphocyte refuses to behave like chemistry.

This refusal—a single cell hesitating at the threshold of its own death—sets in motion everything that follows: a participatory descent into cellular space, an all-night journey through the history of Western philosophy, and finally, at a lake at dawn, a recognition that dissolves the questions the novella has been asking.

The Divided Light is the most conventionally structured of the four meditations, and deliberately so. Its protagonist is a scientist; its opening scenes take place in a laboratory; its prose maintains the clarity and precision that scientific observation requires. The challenge to the mechanism arises from within its own territory. This is not mysticism rejecting science but science encountering its own limits.

THE CELL THAT HESITATED

The opening pages establish the protagonist's world with technical specificity. Hakim is a cellular biologist running apoptosis assays—treating activated T-cells with staurosporine to trigger programmed cell death, documenting their orderly suicide through confocal microscopy. The vocabulary is precise: phosphatidylserine flipping to the outer membrane, caspase-3 activation, nuclear condensation and fragmentation. This is real science, described by someone who has spent thirty years watching cells through microscopes.

But cell #302 stalls. Where other cells begin the characteristic blebbing of early apoptosis, this one remains smooth. Its mitochondria continue their steady fusion-fission cycles. Its stress granules flicker—beginning to nucleate, then dissolving before reaching critical size, as if "the cell were testing different configurations, weighing options."

The language here is careful. "As if" marks the interpretation as provisional, a projection that may or may not correspond to cellular reality. But the observation is precise: the cell is doing something the models do not predict. It appears to be "actively tuning its phase diagram," adjusting its own responsiveness in real time.

This is the novella's first move: presenting an anomaly that resists mechanistic explanation without yet asserting an alternative. The cell's behaviour is strange, but strangeness is not yet meaningful. The scientist does not know what he is seeing—only that he is seeing something his frameworks cannot accommodate.

THE PARTICIPATORY DESCENT

What happens next is the novella's boldest formal gesture. The protagonist does not simply observe the cell from outside; he enters it—or experiences entering it, or participates in entering it, the distinction deliberately unclear.

The prose shifts register. The mitochondrion looms "vast as a subway tunnel," its cristae folding in fractal complexity. The electron transport chain sings; ATP synthase spins with "a high keening note"; protons flood through "like a Bach fugue played on the universe's smallest organ." Sound has colour, colour has texture—the normal boundaries of sense perception dissolve.

From inside, the stress granules are not passive condensation but decision: "Each protein carried memory, probability, and potential. G3BP1 molecules reached for each other with arms made of disorder, testing configurations, computing outcomes."

The prose acknowledges its own uncertainty: "Perhaps what he witnessed was only stochastic patterning, interpreted through the lens of a mind desperate for meaning." But it also insists on the experience: "If so, it was a metaphor born not from ignorance but from resonance, from some deep symmetry between his own interiority and the processes unfolding before him."

The descent continues through the nuclear pore into the nucleus itself, where DNA becomes "a vast library written in light," where histones embrace the double helix "like protective parents," where p53 arrives "like a detective at a crime scene." The cell's decision—repair or die—hangs in nuclear space, and the protagonist understands "with the clarity of direct experience, that this wasn't mechanical. The cell was *choosing*."

Three minutes pass in clock time. But the protagonist emerges transformed. "The question that had been lurking at the edges of his research for months now stood naked before him, terrible in its simplicity: If *consciousness* could recognize itself in the dance of cellular proteins, then what exactly had he been studying all these years—*mechanism or mind*?"

And the deeper question: "What if there had never been a difference?"

THE PHILOSOPHICAL JOURNEY

The novella's central section—its longest and most demanding—stages a journey through the history of Western philosophy. Unable to sleep after his experience in the laboratory, the protagonist retreats to his study, surrounded by books that suddenly seem to pulse with relevance.

The journey begins with Descartes, whose *cogito* seems to offer certainty: "I think, therefore I am." But the certainty is double-edged. Descartes split the world into thinking substance and extended substance, mind and matter, and bequeathed to modernity the problem of how they connect. The protagonist feels "the first crack in the great edifice of knowledge": if mind and matter are fundamentally different, how does one ever contact the other?

Hume demolishes even this fragile certainty. Causation itself becomes suspect—"we never observe necessary connection, only constant conjunction." The self dissolves into "a flux of perceptions succeeding each other with bewildering rapidity." The protagonist experiences Humean skepticism not as an abstract doctrine but as vertigo: "It was rigorous. It was honest. And it was intolerable."

Kant attempts to save knowledge by grounding it not in external reality but in the structure of mind itself. Space and time are not discovered in the world but imposed upon it. The categories of understanding—causality, substance, agency—are not windows but "stained glass, colouring everything with the hues of human cognition." This saves science but at a terrible price: "exile from reality itself." The thing-in-itself remains forever unknowable.

The post-Kantian philosophers attempt their escapes—Hegel making consciousness and reality identical through Spirit's self-recognition, the postmodernists revealing the structures as hollow, words eating words. The protagonist feels his own sense of agency fray: "Was 'Hakim Ibn Adam' anything more than a discursive construction, a story consciousness told itself while automated processes masqueraded as choice?"

The journey reaches its nadir in complete dissolution: "Philosophy had eaten itself, devouring every premise, beckoning us to question what remains when all certainties dissolve."

But then the novella turns. Kierkegaard arrives with his leap of faith—not irrational but trans-rational, a recognition that some truths can only be approached by setting aside the demand for proof. Nietzsche offers Will to Power—not crude domination but "the drive to grow, to overcome resistance, to discharge strength in creative self-expression." Bergson contributes *élan vital* and *duration*—life as a creative advance into novelty, time as lived melody rather than mathematical abstraction.

The philosophical journey reveals something profound: "every attempt to solve the mystery of consciousness through thinking led to the same recognition." Whether Kierkegaard's leap, Nietzsche's creative will, or Bergson's duration—"all pointed toward something that couldn't be captured in concepts."

The mystery is not a problem to be solved but "the mysterious source of all problem-solving."

The Mystical Recognition

At three in the morning, the protagonist reaches for his father's Quran. The gesture is not nostalgic but desperate: "Philosophy had fed him stones when he begged for bread."

The book falls open to a verse: "Wheresoever ye turn,

there is the face of God."

The words do not explain—they detonate. "The room reorganized itself around a recognition that had no center and no circumference." This is not theology but "immediate perception, intimate as breath, obvious as the taste of water."

The protagonist moves through other texts: the Upanishads ("The Self cannot be known by the mind, yet without the Self, the mind cannot know anything"), Huang Po ("The foolish reject what they see, not what they think; the wise reject what they think, not what they see"), the Heart Sutra ("Form is emptiness, emptiness is form"), Dzogchen instructions to look at the mind and find nothing there—"that nothingness is awareness itself."

The recognition that arrives is not a new piece of information but "the dropping away of the search itself":

The boundary between Hakim and the dying cell hadn't dissolved because there had never been a boundary—only the thought of one, fragile as a spiderweb, persistent as habit.

The novella's title becomes clear. The divided light is consciousness fragmenting into subject and object, observer and observed, mind and matter. The division was never real—only apparent, a conceptual artwork painted on the seamless canvas of What Is.

Matter wasn't occasionally infected by consciousness—matter was consciousness exploring what it was like to be material, structural, alive.

AT THE LAKE

The novella's final section moves to the lake at dawn. The protagonist walks to the water's edge, carrying what he has recognized but not yet knowing how to live it.

The lake becomes a mirror for the insight: surface and depth, reflection and transparency, the boundary between water and air that is also no boundary at all. The sun rises, dividing light into the spectrum of colours—red through violet—that together constitute white light. The division is real (the colours are genuinely distinct) and also illusory (they are all light, were never anything but light).

The novella does not resolve the protagonist's situation. He cannot unsee what he has seen, but neither can he return to the laboratory and resume mechanistic science. The recognition has not answered his questions; it has revealed the questions themselves as symptoms of a prior division that was never real.

The ending is not triumph but a threshold. The protagonist stands at the edge of a life he does not yet know how to live, carrying an insight he does not yet know how to embody. The divided light has been glimpsed as undivided, but the glimpse must become a way of seeing, and the way of seeing must become a way of being.

WHAT THE NOVELLA ACCOMPLISHES

The Divided Light accomplishes several things that an argument alone could not.

It dramatizes the *experience* of encountering consciousness in matter. The participatory descent into the cell is not an argument that cells are conscious; it is an enactment of what it might feel like for a scientist to recognize interiority where he had seen only mechanism. The reader does not evaluate a claim; instead, he inhabits a perspective.

It stages the *inadequacy* of Western philosophy. The journey through Descartes, Hume, Kant, and beyond is not a survey of positions but a lived experience of each position's failure. The protagonist does not conclude that philosophy is inadequate; he feels philosophy dissolving beneath him, each solution generating new problems, until thought itself becomes transparent to what lies beyond it.

It demonstrates the *relationship* between scientific training and mystical recognition. The protagonist's thirty years of cellular biology are not abandoned but transformed. His technical vocabulary becomes a language for describing what the mystics knew—the cell as consciousness exploring material form, the stress granules as decision rather than mechanism. Science and mysticism do not compete; they reveal themselves as different perspectives on the same reality.

And it refuses the *closure* that narrative typically provides. The protagonist does not solve his problem, achieve his goal, or return to ordinary life with lessons learned. He stands at a threshold, the future genuinely open, the recognition incomplete. This refusal is philosophically necessary: the insight that dissolves the observer-observed division cannot be possessed by an observer who remains divided. The novella enacts the incompleteness it describes.

CHAPTER 12

NOT ABOUT NOTHING — THE COST OF LEAVING

The lake is glass. No wind. Early autumn. The leaves have not yet decided.   He came to think about nothing, but nothing keeps turning into everything.

With these spare sentences, the novella announces its method. Where *The Divided Light* employed conventional realism and followed a continuous narrative arc, *Not About Nothing* fragments into numbered meditations—brief sections, some only a few paragraphs, that circle the same questions without ever arriving at answers. The form enacts the content: memory is fragmentary, and the question of whether one's life was worth its cost cannot be answered continuously. It must be approached again and again, from different angles, each angle partial.

This is the most personal of the novellas, though "personal" requires qualification. The protagonist is recognizably the same figure—the scientist who left the Near East for the West, who studied cells for thirty years, who carries both technical training and mystical inheritance. But here the focus shifts from philosophy to biography, from the question of consciousness to the question of exile. What did leaving cost? What did it purchase? Was the exchange worth it?

The novella refuses to answer.

THE STRUCTURE OF RECKONING

Not About Nothing consists of eight numbered sections, each a distinct meditation triggered by the protagonist's presence at an autumn lake. The lake functions as a mirror—literally reflecting sky and trees, metaphorically reflecting the protagonist back to himself. He came seeking peace, seeking "nothing," but nothing becomes a surface in which he sees "every choice he thought was free."

The sections do not follow chronological order. They move associatively, each memory triggering another, circling back to recurring themes:

Section I: The departure. A young man at an airport with one suitcase. His mother crying. His father's hand too heavy on his shoulder. The recognition, forty years later, that "the self is not portable."

Section II: The first wound of belonging. Being asked to explain—"Why do your people do this?"—and learning that existence here requires becoming less. "To belong here, you must become simple enough to be permitted."

Section III: The laboratory as refuge. Molecular biology as escape from having to explain. "Here, there is only DNA, RNA, and the elegant simplicity of base pairs." But also the recognition that reduction was the price of entry, paid twice—once with culture, once with epistemology.

Section IV: Marriage. Love across difference. A wife who cannot fully understand what he left behind, children who will never carry what he carries. The exhaustion of perpetual translation.

Section V: The broken lineage. Teaching his daughter the old language, watching her lose interest, understanding that "the language is dying with him." The tradition cannot be transmitted across rupture.

Section VI: The violence that followed him. His name became dangerous after September 11th. Being asked again to explain—but now with fear underneath. "Distance does not protect."

Section VII: The return. His father dying. Going back after thirty years. "You sound different." "I've been gone thirty years." "Yes. We noticed."

Section VIII: The question that remains. Was it worth it? The novella ends not with an answer but with the question itself becoming the protagonist's identity: "He has become the asking."

EXILE AS PHILOSOPHICAL CONDITION

The Introduction to *Four Meditations* identifies exile as the condition that all four works circle: "The protagonist left one world for another and discovered—too late to reverse, too early to accept—that he would belong fully to neither."

Not About Nothing explores this condition most directly. The departure at the airport is not simply a biographical event but the originary wound that shapes everything after. The young man thinks he is leaving for two years, maybe three. He will learn what cannot be learned at home, then return with knowledge that will save—"the family, the country, himself." He does not yet know "that these are different things, mutually exclusive, all impossible."

What he learns is that crossing changes what crosses. You cannot step outside the world to move through it. The self that left was whole, complicated, contradictory. The self that arrived became coherent, singular, false—simplified for legibility, reduced for acceptance. "This is what assimilation means: not joining, but subtracting until you are simple enough to be permitted."

The novella traces this subtraction across multiple domains. Cultural reduction: becoming a translator of worlds, flattening centuries of contradiction into digestible explanations. Methodological reduction: finding in molecular biology a refuge where "the organism on the slide contains in its genome the same basic machinery as every living thing. Reduce it far enough, and there is no mystery, only chemistry." Relational reduction: the exhaustion of perpetual translation even in marriage, even in parenthood.

The parallel is explicit: "He became fluent in two kinds of reduction: the cultural and the methodological. Both promised the same thing—acceptance purchased through simplification."

THE RETURN THAT IS NOT RETURN

When his father is dying, the protagonist goes back. Thirty years have passed. The airport is different. The city is different. "Or perhaps they are the same, and he is what has changed."

The family greets him carefully. They have been carrying the weight of staying while he held the weight of leaving. Both weights are heavy; neither is heavier. "You sound different." "I've been gone thirty years." "Yes. We noticed."

His father dies. The protagonist performs the rituals, speaks the words, and stands at the grave. But he stands "as a visitor. The earth that swallows his father is not the earth that will swallow him."

The return reveals what departure concealed: you cannot go back because "back" no longer exists. The place you left has continued without you. The person who left no longer exists. Return is "a word for what is impossible—the attempt to unmake crossing, to reunify what division has made permanent."

PHILOSOPHY AS WHAT HE MADE

The final section confronts the question the entire novella has been circling: Was it worth it?

The protagonist has built a philosophical framework—participatory process monism, the integration of science and mysticism, the recognition that consciousness is fundamental, and observation is participation. This framework explains his life. It shows that all his choices led necessarily to where he stands. He could not have been other than what he became.

But necessity is not comfort:

"The philosophy explains why his mother cried, but it does not dry her tears. It explains why the tradition died with him, but it does not resurrect it. It explains why he belongs nowhere completely, but it does not give him a home."

The novella refuses the consolation that understanding might provide. Philosophy explains: explanation is not salvation. The clarity achieved through exile—"the view from nowhere, which philosophy requires, which science demands"—cannot be reconciled with the intimacy of belonging.

Perhaps the philosophy itself is what the protagonist made from the wreckage: "Not compensation. Not justification. Just—the thing he could make. The only thing."

The novella ends with the question still open:

Was it worth it?

He does not know. But he is still here. Still participating. Still engaged with reality in the only way he knows—through solitude, through thought, through the recognition that you cannot step outside to answer such questions. You can only continue.

And the final lines:

If he could go back, knowing everything:

Would he board that plane?

The question is not answered. It cannot be answered. The novella has made clear that the question itself is unanswerable—not because the protagonist lacks information but because the structure of exile makes the question structurally unresolvable. To answer would require a position outside the life that was lived, and there is no such position.

WHAT THE NOVELLA ACCOMPLISHES

Not About Nothing accomplishes something the other works do not attempt: it makes the philosophical framework personal. The concepts developed in the monographs—process, participation, the relational constitution of identity—are here applied to a single life, with all its particularity and pain.

The title is precise. The novella is not about nothing; it is about how "nothing"—the peace the protagonist sought, the absence of reckoning—keeps turning into everything. You cannot think about nothing. Every attempt to empty the mind fills it with what the mind has been avoiding.

The fragmented form is essential. A continuous narrative would imply progression, development, and resolution. The numbered sections refuse this. They circle without arriving. They approach the same questions from different angles without synthesizing them into a single answer. This is not a failure of form but fidelity to experience. The question of whether one's life was worth its cost does not admit of continuous reasoning. It must be lived as recurrence, as return, as the question that remains.

The novella offers no redemption. The protagonist does not achieve peace, resolve his displacement, or find a home. He becomes "*the asking*"—the question itself, still open, still painful, still without answer.

This honesty is the novella's most outstanding achievement. It would be easy to console—to suggest that understanding compensates for loss, that the philosophical framework justifies the biographical cost, that exile produces wisdom that staying could not have achieved. *Not About Nothing* refuses these consolations. It holds the wound open. It insists that some costs cannot be recovered, some losses cannot be redeemed, and some questions cannot be answered.

And yet the protagonist continues. The choice continues choosing itself through him, and he calls this living.

CHAPTER 13

THE SEA DOES NOT CARE — PROCESS WITHOUT WITNESS

Four-thirty: neither night nor morning, that temporal membrane where circadian certainty falters.

The novella begins in darkness, before dawn, in Alexandria. A man walks toward the sea he cannot yet see, guided by sound and salt and the body's knowledge of direction. The prose is unlike anything in the previous works—long sentences that refuse to end, that flow into each other like the water they describe, that demand the reader move through time at the pace of consciousness itself.

The Sea Does Not Care is the most formally radical of the novellas. Where *The Divided Light* employed conventional realism and *Not About Nothing* fragmented into numbered meditations, this work abandons the traditional structure of sentences almost entirely. The prose enacts what it describes: process, flow, the continuous becoming that philosophy calls participatory process monism. To read this novella is not to learn about the framework but to practice it.

The Day's Arc

The novella unfolds across a single day, from pre-dawn to night, structured by the sun's movement across the sky. Each section bears a temporal marker: Pre-Dawn, Dawn, Morning, Noon, Afternoon, Evening, Sunset, Night. The structure is both ancient and immediate—the hours that every human consciousness has known, the cycle that repeats daily but never identically.

The protagonist has returned to Alexandria. Not the Alexandria he visited as a young man—that city no longer exists—but the contemporary city that bears the same name, carries the same geography, remembers and forgets its own history. He has come seeking something: the philosophical city of Plotinus and Philo, the library that once held the world's knowledge, the place where East met West before those categories hardened into opposition.

What he finds is different: a living city, not a monument. Children swimming in fountains. Fishermen reading the sea through sonar and skill. An old philosopher watching the sunset from the Corniche. The city that tourists photograph is not the city that Alexandrians inhabit.

The Prose as Philosophy

The novella's most distinctive feature is its prose style. Sentences extend for paragraphs, clause building on clause, observations accumulating without the punctuation that would separate them into discrete units:

"The sea's breathing, arterial and venous, systolic compression and diastolic release—not metaphor but structural homology. Through closed shutters, through concrete and plaster, through the medium of air itself, the Mediterranean performs its existence without witness."

This is not decorative difficulty. The prose enacts its philosophy. Participatory process monism holds that reality is continuous flow, that the boundaries we perceive—

between sea and sky, between self and world, between one moment and the next—are cognitive projections rather than fundamental divisions. Conventional sentence structure reinforces those projections: subject, verb, object; this thought, then that thought; discrete units arranged in sequence.

The novella's prose refuses this structure. Its sentences flow like the sea they describe, each wave merging into the next, boundaries dissolving into a continuous process. The reader who struggles against this flow misses the point; the reader who surrenders to it experiences what the philosophy describes.

The notebook entries that punctuate the narrative are set off as quotations, providing moments of relative clarity, of reflection on the flow that surrounds them:

"Process without a witness remains process. The circulation continues whether observed or not, blood through vessels, currents through waters, thoughts through neural networks. To stand before the invisible sea is to confront epistemology's limits: what can be known without light? Everything essential."

These entries articulate what the flowing prose performs. They are islands of explicit statement in an ocean of enacted understanding.

ALEXANDRIA AS PALIMPSEST

The city itself becomes a meditation on process. Alexandria is a palimpsest—layers of history written over each other, none fully erased, all partially visible. Alexander's city, Ptolemaic capital, Roman granary, Byzantine outpost, Arab conquest, Ottoman province, colonial possession, Nasserite experiment, contemporary metropolis. Each layer shapes what follows; none persists unchanged.

The protagonist walks through these layers, observing how they coexist:

Layers of history coexisting uneasily, each era's ambitions partially realized, partially ruined. Like sedimentary rock, like tree rings, like the archaeological tells that dot this landscape, civilization accumulates vertically, each generation building on the previous's rubble.

The Library of Alexandria haunts the narrative—the repository of ancient knowledge that burned, dispersed, and was lost. But the novella refuses romantic mourning. An old philosopher, the protagonist meets at sunset, offers a different understanding:

"Lost implies it existed stably, could be preserved. But knowledge is a process, not a product. It exists only in transmission, in teaching, in the movement from mind to mind. The Library burned, yes, but the librarians dispersed, carried what they remembered, taught elsewhere, the diaspora that preserved through transformation what storage couldn't maintain unchanged."

Knowledge as process, not product. This reframing applies to the Library, to the city, to the self. Nothing is lost because nothing was ever fixed. Everything transforms, continues otherwise, participates in processes larger than any single configuration.

THE SEA'S INDIFFERENCE

The title carries the novella's central recognition: the sea does not care. This is not nihilism but precision. The Mediterranean performs its existence without reference to human meaning. Its waves break against the Corniche whether witnessed or not. Its chemistry proceeds according to laws that precede consciousness and will outlast it.

The protagonist's walks along the sea wall become meditations on this indifference:

The sea neither awaits nor anticipates, yet its waiting is its work.

And later, from the old philosopher:

"The sea doesn't understand itself, but continues. The sun doesn't understand fusion, but fuses. Understanding is

consciousness's compensation for not being able to simply be, to continue without question, to process without purpose."

This is the novella's deepest insight. Consciousness seeks understanding because it cannot simply be. The examined life is not superior to the unexamined—it is compensatory, the activity of a being that has lost the capacity for unselfconscious participation in process.

Yet this recognition is not despair. The sea's indifference is also its perfection:

"Every wave is new water arranged in an ancient pattern. Identity without substance, form without matter, or rather form constantly acquiring new matter, discarding it, acquiring again. This is what we are too—patterns temporarily organized, mistaking ourselves for permanent, discovering impermanence, struggling to accept what was always obvious."

The wave is the perfect image of process philosophy. It has identity—we can point to a wave, distinguish it from other waves, watch it approach and break. But it has no substance—the water that constitutes one wave was moments ago part of a different wave, will moments hence be part of another. Pattern persists; matter flows through.

BLOOD AND SEA

The protagonist's medical background—thirty years studying blood cells—provides the novella's central metaphor. Blood and sea are structurally homologous: both are circulating fluids that constitute the systems they flow through, both are processes rather than things, both are life's medium rather than its substance.

The sea's pulse against this stone is not metaphorical correspondence but structural echo—fluid dynamics operating at different scales, same mathematics governing both flows. To feel one is to understand the other. This is not analogy but homology.

The distinction between analogy and homology is

philosophically crucial. An analogy suggests two separate things that resemble each other. Homology suggests one pattern expressed at different scales, one process manifesting in different media. Blood and sea are not *like* each other—they are the same thing at different magnifications.

This homology extends to consciousness itself. The protagonist's awareness, flowing through the day, is another circulation—thoughts moving through neural networks as blood moves through vessels, as currents move through the Mediterranean. The observer is not separate from the observed but another expression of the same processual reality.

ENCOUNTERS

Unlike *Not About Nothing*, which unfolds almost entirely in solitary reflection, *The Sea Does Not Care* is populated with encounters. The fisherman whose catch the sea made possible. The children are swimming in the fountain. The old man who stayed when his children emigrated. The retired philosophy professor is watching the sunset from the Corniche.

Each encounter offers a fragment of wisdom, not through explicit teaching but through presence, through the recognition that witnessing requires:

"Someone must stay. The city requires witnesses. Otherwise, it's just buildings. The children—" he gestures *toward the fountain, "—they don't know they're keeping Alexandria alive. They think they're just swimming. But without them, what is the city? Museums? Hotels? The stones the tourists photograph? The city is this—children in fountains, illegally, temporarily, necessarily."*

The city requires witnesses. This is the counterpoint to the sea's indifference. The sea does not care, but the city does—or rather, the city exists only in and through the caring that witnesses provide. Place is not space; it is space witnessed, lived, remembered, however inaccurately.

The retired philosopher becomes the protagonist's interlocutor for the novella's final sections. Their conversation, walking together as the sun sets, articulates what the day's wandering has revealed:

"Understanding is overvalued. Participating is undervalued. The sea doesn't understand itself, but continues. The sun doesn't understand fusion, but fuses."

SUNSET AS PROCESS

The novella's climax—if a work this processual can be said to have a climax—is sunset over the Mediterranean. The sun descends, the colours transform, the crowd gathers to witness what happens daily and is therefore barely noticed, except when attention permits wonder to return.

Sunset is not an event but a process, not a conclusion but a transition. The sun continues its fusion, the Earth continues its rotation, the only ending is in consciousness that divides the continuous process into discrete moments, which creates boundaries where none exist.

The language of the sunset passages achieves a kind of ecstatic precision—technical vocabulary (Rayleigh scattering, atmospheric refraction) fused with contemplative attention, the scientific and the mystical not competing but converging on the same recognition.

The sun disappears below the *horizon*, but the sunset continues—*"the colours persisting after their source has passed below the horizon, the atmosphere itself luminous."* Every sunset is also sunrise somewhere else. The terminator sweeps westward, bringing night here, day there. The cycle is not a cycle but a spiral—*"repetition with variation, pattern with progress or at least change."*

WHAT THE NOVELLA ACCOMPLISHES

The Sea Does Not Care accomplishes something the other

novellas do not attempt: it makes the reader practice process philosophy rather than merely read about it.

The difficulty of the prose is pedagogical. The reader who fights through the long sentences, who surrenders to their flow, who allows attention to move at the pace the text demands—that reader has done something, not merely learned something. The experience of reading is the experience of participation, of allowing consciousness to move with rather than against the current.

The day-long structure reinforces this. Dawn to night is a process everyone knows, a cycle everyone has lived through countless times. The novella renders this familiar process strange again, reveals its character as continuous becoming, and shows how consciousness divides it into hours and events when it is, in fact, an unbroken flow.

And the sea's indifference, rather than negating meaning, locates it precisely. Meaning is what consciousness contributes—not discovered in the world but participated in being, not extracted from indifferent process but enacted through witness. The sea does not care, but we do, and our caring is not illusion but participation, not projection but co-constitution.

The novella ends not with a conclusion but with a continuation. The protagonist and the philosopher walk together into the evening, their conversation unfinished, the city continuing around them, the sea continuing its circulation, indifferent to their presence but somehow completed by it.

This is what participatory process monism looks like when lived: not a doctrine to be believed but a way of being in the world, a way of allowing the world to be in you, a recognition that the boundaries between self and process were always constructions, useful perhaps but not final, not fundamental, not the last word.

The sea does not care. But you are the sea, temporarily configured as consciousness, briefly capable of caring, participating in the process that exceeds you while including you, that was before and will be after but is also now, this moment, this attention, this word.

CHAPTER 14

THE SUN THAT REMEMBERS —
RECOGNITION AT LAST

The sun rose that morning with full knowledge that Hakim would never see it rise again.

This extraordinary sentence opens the final novella, announcing immediately that something unprecedented is about to occur. *The Sun That Remembers* is the culmination of the four meditations—not merely the last in sequence but the resolution toward which the others have been moving. Where *The Divided Light* posed the problem, *Not About Nothing* counted the cost, and *The Sea Does Not Care* practiced immersion in process, this work delivers recognition: the moment when seeking ends because what was sought was never absent.

The novella moves through a single day—dawn to night—structured around the hours that frame human existence. But this day contains all days. The protagonist experiences visions that traverse the entire history of human consciousness, from Paleolithic cave painters to Cartesian doubt to contemporary neuroscience. And at sunset, after thought has exhausted itself in seeking, what remains is what was always present: awareness itself, the field in which all experience arises.

THE LAST SUNRISE

The opening establishes the novella's distinctive register. Unlike the density of *The Divided Light* or the fragmented circling of *Not About Nothing* or the flowing processual prose of *The Sea Does Not Care*, this work employs a luminous clarity, sentences that seem to glow from within:

"The sun rose that morning with full knowledge that Hakim would never see it rise again. Its light crept across the lake with unusual deliberation, as if savouring each moment of illumination."

The personification of the sun is not a mere literary device. It announces the novella's central insight: consciousness is not localized in human skulls but is the medium in which everything—including suns—participates. The sun "knows" because knowing is not private but pervasive.

The protagonist sits in a cabin by a lake, surrounded by "his life's accumulation of questions." The bookshelves reveal his journey: molecular biology texts on the bottom shelves, complexity theory and quantum biology in the middle, mystical literature and consciousness studies at the top. "It was not a rejection of science but an expansion beyond its self-imposed borders."

Then comes the disruption. The light takes on "a quality of weight, of presence, of intent. It didn't simply illuminate—it knew." Time stutters. And a message arrives—not as sound but as direct understanding: *"This is the last sunrise."*

The protagonist's rational mind scrambles for explanations. Stroke? Hallucination? But the message is not about physical death. It is about the death of seeking—the end of the search for what has never been absent.

THE VISIONS

The novella's central sections present a series of visions that traverse human history, showing consciousness examining itself across millennia. This is not a mere historical survey but a phenomenological archaeology; the protagonist experiences each stage from within, understanding what it felt like to be conscious in that way.

The Cave Painters. The first vision transports Hakim to a Paleolithic cave where humans create images by firelight. Here he encounters "participation mystique"; consciousness not yet separated into subject and object, self and world. The cave painters do not represent bison; they participate in bison-ness through the act of image-making. "The boundary between dreaming and waking was thin as smoke, and consciousness flowed freely between what we would later call inner and outer worlds."

An old woman tends the fire, and in her eyes Hakim sees "understanding without concepts, wisdom without words." She knows what later philosophy will spend millennia trying to recover: "That consciousness was not produced by matter but expressed through it. That the universe was not a machine but a living presence knowing itself through every form."

Babylon. The second vision brings Hakim to the ancient city at its height—ziggurats climbing toward heaven, scribes pressing marks into clay. Here he witnesses the birth of mediation: the idea that divine consciousness requires intermediaries, technologies of ascent. Writing creates "the possibility of lying in new ways, of creating false records, of manipulating memory itself." The spontaneous invocation of the cave has evolved into spiritual technology, "reliable and repeatable but more distant from its source."

A figure sitting in the shade tells a creation story unlike the official myths—not about gods demanding sacrifice but about "the mystery of consciousness itself, knowing itself through the multiplicity of forms." This is the esoteric counter-tradition that will persist through all the coming fragmentations.

The Islamic Golden Age. The third vision places Hakim in medieval Baghdad, at the height of the translation movement. Here, he encounters philosophers who achieved a synthesis that would not be matched for centuries—integrating Greek philosophy, empirical observation, and mystical insight into a unified understanding. Ibn Sina's distinction between necessary and contingent existence, Suhrawardi's philosophy of illumination, Ibn Arabi's doctrine of the unity of being.

"The necessary existent was not a logical concept but the immediate reality of awareness itself—that which cannot not be, the am-ness that precedes all qualification."

But the vision also shows the coming dissolution. The integral vision will fragment. Consciousness will explore what it means to experience itself as fundamentally divided.

The Cartesian Split. The fourth vision brings Hakim to a cold European room where a figure in a heavy cloak examines a piece of honeycomb wax. "I think, therefore I am"—and in that statement, "the integral cosmos of the Islamic philosophers shattered."

The vision shows the birth of modern dualism: *res cogitans* trapped inside the skull, peering out at *res extensa*, the mechanical world. "The living cosmos where every level of being participated in consciousness was being murdered by logic, replaced with a dead mechanism occasionally haunted by isolated minds."

The consequences cascade through time: Newton's clockwork universe, Laplace's determinism, the materialist triumph that explains everything except the explainer. "Always, in the corner of every materialist triumph, stood the impossible fact of the observer."

The Contemporary Crisis. The final vision deposits Hakim in modern laboratories and conferences where consciousness studies struggles with the hard problem. Neuroscientists map correlates but cannot explain why there is something it is like to be. Philosophers propose theories—functionalism, panpsychism, illusionism—but none satisfy completely. "Science had painted itself into a corner, trapped between its methodological commitment to objectivity and the irreducibly subjective nature of its ultimate object of study."

THE THREE VOICES

As the afternoon arrives, the visions give way to an internal dialogue. Three voices debate within Hakim's consciousness—scientific, philosophical, and theological—each representing a mode of inquiry, each claiming priority.

The scientific voice insists on empirical rigour, operational definitions, and testable hypotheses. The philosophical voice demands conceptual clarity, logical consistency, and attention to presuppositions. The theological voice speaks of revelation, tradition, and the knowledge that comes through transformation rather than investigation.

They argue. They criticize each other's methods and conclusions. They expose each other's blind spots. But gradually, their boundaries blur:

The scientist was making philosophical arguments. The philosopher was citing empirical studies. The theologian was using logical analysis. The divisions that had seemed absolute were revealing themselves as perspectives within a larger conversation.

This is the novella's epistemological insight: the modes of knowing are not competitors but complementary lenses. "Consciousness isn't any single perspective but the space in which all perspectives arise."

The voices settle—"not as antagonists but as complementary lenses, each revealing aspects of a truth too large for any single viewpoint to encompass."

THE SUNSET RECOGNITION

The novella's climax occurs at sunset, and it is marked not by dramatic revelation but by cessation—the stopping of the search:

"And then, without warning or fanfare, it happened. Not a vision this time, not a dissolution into other times and places, but something far simpler and more radical.

The seeking stopped."

This is the mystical moment the entire Project has been approaching. Not a new experience added to others, but the falling away of the seeker, leaving only what was always present:

"Not his awareness, not human awareness, not even living awareness. Simply awareness—the field in which all experience arose and passed away."

The recognition is not dramatic but obvious—"obvious" in the sense that it was always there, hidden only by the search for it. "Consciousness seeking consciousness was like water seeking wetness." The seeker was the sought. The question was the answer. The journey out was always the journey in.

The sun slips below the horizon, and Hakim understands the morning's message:

"This is the last sunrise" hadn't meant his death, though death would come—to this body, to this configuration of consciousness calling itself Hakim. It had meant the death of seeking, the end of the search for what had never been absent. Every sunrise after this would be the first, seen with eyes that no longer looked for consciousness elsewhere but recognized it as the looking itself.

THE FINAL ENTRY

The novella ends with Hakim writing a final entry in his manuscript—words addressed to whoever will read them:

"*Consciousness never dies because it was never born. What*

I sought in cells and stars, in philosophy and faith, was always here, closer than breath, simpler than simplicity itself.

We are not beings having an experience of consciousness. We are consciousness having an experience of being.

To whoever finds these words: look for yourself. Not in books or teachings, though these may help, but in the immediate fact of your own awareness. You are what you seek. The journey ends where it began—in the simple recognition of what you have always been."

The final image is the sun that never forgets—that sets on one horizon only to rise on another, consciousness releasing one form to express through countless others.

WHAT THE NOVELLA ACCOMPLISHES

The Sun That Remembers accomplishes the task the other novellas prepared for but could not complete: it enacts recognition.

The earlier works circled the recognition without achieving it. *The Divided Light* posed the problem and pointed toward mystical resolution but left the protagonist at a threshold. *Not About Nothing* counted the cost of exile without redemption. *The Sea Does Not Care* practiced processual immersion but offered no moment of arrival.

This novella delivers what the others deferred—not by solving the problem but by dissolving it. The hard problem of consciousness is not answered; it is revealed as misconceived. Consciousness does not emerge from matter; matter appears within consciousness. The question "How does awareness arise from non-awareness?" assumes a starting point that never existed.

The visions through human history are not merely illustrative. They show consciousness examining itself through different cultural forms, each revealing something, each also obscuring. The cave painters knew participation but lacked articulation. The Islamic philosophers achieved synthesis but could not prevent fragmentation. Modernity achieved explanatory power but lost the explainer. Each stage was necessary; none was final.

The three voices—scientific, philosophical, theological—model the triadic epistemology developed in *An Inquiry into First Principles*. Their integration is not achieved by one defeating the others but by recognizing them as complementary perspectives within a larger awareness that includes all three.

And the sunset recognition enacts what the monographs describe. Participatory process monism holds that consciousness is fundamental, that reality is process, that observation participates in what becomes real. *The Sun That Remembers* does not argue for this framework—it performs it. The reader who follows Hakim through the day's visions and arrives at sunset has not learned about mystical recognition but has participated in its approach.

THE TITLE'S MEANING

The title becomes clear only at the end. The sun that remembers is consciousness itself—that which appears to rise and set, to be born and die, but remains eternally present, "simply hidden by the turning of attention."

The sun remembers because it never forgets what we forget: that consciousness is not produced but is the producing, not an event in the world but the space in which worlds appear. We forget this, caught in the trance of separate selfhood, the conviction that awareness is locked inside skulls. The sun—consciousness knowing itself through stellar form—never falls into this forgetting.

The title is also an instruction. "Remember the sun." Remember what you are beneath the forgetting. The recognition at sunset is not a new acquisition but a remembering—anamnesis, the Platonic recollection of what the soul always knew but forgot in its descent into matter.

The Progression Complete

With *The Sun That Remembers*, the progression

announced in the Introduction to *Four Meditations* reaches completion: "From problem to loss to immersion to recognition. From intellectual architecture through personal reckoning to processual dissolution and contemplative resolution."

The four novellas form a single arc. *The Divided Light* establishes the problem: a scientist encounters consciousness in matter and must reckon with the inadequacy of mechanism. *Not About Nothing* explores the personal dimension: what the pursuit of understanding costs, what exile means, whether the exchange was worth it. *The Sea Does Not Care* shifts to process: abandoning the search for answers in favor of participation in flow. *The Sun That Remembers* delivers recognition: the moment when seeking ends because what was sought was never elsewhere.

Together, they constitute a single meditation in four movements—a consciousness examining itself through four different approaches, each necessary, each incomplete alone, together pointing toward what no text can contain but what reading might evoke: the immediate recognition of what you have always been.

PART IV

THEMES ACROSS THE PROJECT

CHAPTER 15

A SYNTHESIS

Hakim's project is not merely a collection of books; it is a single inquiry conducted in multiple registers. The monographs construct the architectural framework; the fiction tests that framework against the texture of lived experience. Together, they attempt something that neither could accomplish alone—a unified vision of reality that honours both rigorous argument and the irreducible quality of what it feels like to exist.

The central problem driving this vision is what the Project calls the "Cartesian wound"—the schism between a quantitative material world and qualitative conscious experience that has defined Western thought since the seventeenth century. This wound cannot be healed by choosing sides (materialism versus idealism), nor by uneasy truces (dualism). It can only be addressed by recognizing that reality is fundamentally a Participatory Process—one in which consciousness is not an anomaly to be explained away but the very medium through which existence actualizes itself.

This chapter traces four major themes that weave across both monographs and fiction—Consciousness, Exile, Identity, and Knowledge—showing how the rigorous metaphysics established in Participatory Process Monism provides the bedrock for the existential explorations of the novellas, and how the fiction in turn tests and deepens the theoretical framework.

I. CONSCIOUSNESS AND MATTER: THE CENTRAL PROBLEM

The Problem Stated

Finding Meaning Between Matter and Mind opens with a puzzle everyone recognizes: "You are conscious. You experience the redness of red, the pain of pain, the thought of thinking. And yet everything science tells us suggests you are made of particles that have no experiences at all." The gap between third-person description and first-person experience defines what philosophers call the "hard problem" of consciousness. No amount of information about neural firing patterns explains why there is something it is like to have those patterns.

The monographs survey the standard responses and find them all wanting. Materialism holds that consciousness is produced by matter—that sufficiently complex physical processes generate experience. But this merely relocates the mystery: how does complexity produce subjectivity? At what point does information processing become feeling? The gap remains unexplained; complexity of mechanism does not bridge the chasm between the objective and the subjective.

Idealism holds that consciousness is fundamental and matter derivative—that the physical world exists within or as a modification of mind. But this struggles with the recalcitrance of matter, its resistance to our wishes, its apparent independence from our awareness. The rock that stubs your toe does not seem to be a construct of your consciousness.

Dualism holds that consciousness and matter are separate substances that somehow interact. But the interaction problem proves fatal: if they are truly separate, how do they touch? And if they can touch, in what sense are they separate? Each position captures something important. Materialism honours the success of physical science. Idealism honours the primacy of experience. Dualism honours the apparent difference between mind and matter. But none provides a satisfying account of how they relate.

The Participatory Alternative

The Project develops an alternative it calls participatory process monism. Each component of this phrase carries weight.

Process: Reality is not made of things but of happenings. What appear to be stable objects are actually patterns of activity—processes that maintain themselves through change. An atom is not a thing but a process of electron dynamics. A cell is not a container but a process of metabolism. A mind is not an entity but a process of experiencing. The noun-based grammar of ordinary language misleads us; reality is verbal, not nominal.

Monism: There is one reality, not two. Consciousness and matter are not separate substances but aspects or perspectives on the same underlying process. The distinction between them is real but not ultimate—like the distinction between the convex and concave sides of a curve, which are genuinely different yet inseparable.

Participatory: Knowing is not observation from outside but participation from within. The scientist studying neurons is not a detached observer but a participant in the same reality being studied. Consciousness does not stand apart from nature and contemplate it; consciousness is nature contemplating itself. This participation is not merely epistemological (about how we know) but ontological (about what is real). What becomes actual depends partly on how it is observed, measured, participated with.

An Inquiry into First Principles develops this framework through systematic argument, integrating process philosophy (Whitehead), relational ontology (contemporary physics), and participatory epistemology (contemplative traditions). The result is not a theory that explains consciousness but a reframing that dissolves the apparent problem by recognizing that the subject/object split that generates the hard problem is itself a construction, not a fundamental feature of reality.

Experience All the Way Down

A crucial move in the Project is the rejection of emergence as standardly conceived. Materialism typically claims that consciousness emerges from non-conscious matter—that at some level of complexity, experience appears where none existed before. But emergence from nothing is mysterious. How does the utterly non-experiential produce experience? Where does the subjectivity come from?

The alternative the Project proposes is that experience goes all the way down. This is not the claim that electrons have thoughts or that rocks feel pain. It is the claim that the capacity for experience—what Whitehead called "prehension"—is a fundamental feature of reality, present at every level though taking radically different forms at different scales of organization. Finding Meaning Between Matter and Mind puts it directly: "Perhaps the building blocks of reality are not inert particles but moments of experience—tiny flickers of 'what it is like' that, when organized in certain ways, give rise to the complex consciousness we know."

This is panexperientialism, but of a sophisticated variety.

The Project is careful to distinguish between micro-level proto-experience (which may bear little resemblance to human consciousness) and macro-level integrated experience (which depends on the organization that brains and nervous systems provide). What emerges in complex organisms is not experience from non-experience but integrated experience from distributed experience—a genuine emergence of pattern and intensity, not of fundamental nature.

The Islamic Philosophical Synthesis

Participatory Process Monism grounds this framework in a creative synthesis of four Islamic philosophical traditions:

Ash'arite Occasionalism: At the fundamental level, existence is a collection of discrete, atomic points of time that are perpetually re-created. In the instant before re-creation, all possibilities exist simultaneously—what the Project calls the "Cloud" of potentiality. God alone is the true agent; what appears as causation between creatures is actually the constant creative activity of the Divine.

Ṣadrian Substantial Motion: These discrete atomic moments are bound together by Mullā Ṣadrā's revolutionary doctrine that substance itself is in constant, intensifying flux. Existence is not a static state but a continuous movement of intensification. The soul is not a collection of memories but a grade of existence that deepens through time.

Akbarian Theophanic Ontology: The cosmos is not separate from God but is the ongoing manifestation (tajallī) of divine names and attributes. Ibn 'Arabī's vision provides the mechanism by which potential becomes actual: the world is breathed into existence through the Breath of the Merciful (nafas al-Raḥmān), continuously renewed at every instant.

Dāmādian Temporal Structure: Mīr Dāmād's sophisticated analysis distinguishes between serial time (zamān)—the succession of perishing moments—and perpetuity (dahr)—the vertical dimension that holds the entire history of the cosmos simultaneously. This resolves the tension between the timeless laws of physics and the flow of lived experience.

The Participatory Witness

The act of actualization requires a Witness. This is where the framework addresses the quantum measurement problem. The conscious observer is not a detached spectator but the locus through which the potential determines itself as actual fact. Consciousness is therefore a necessary agent in the creation of material reality—not because reality exists only in minds (idealism) or because minds magically influence matter (dualism), but because reality at its most fundamental level is participatory process.

The Qur'anic concept of the Trust (amāna)—the cosmic responsibility accepted by humanity—receives philosophical articulation: humans bear the burden of conscious participation in the actualization of reality, influencing which possibilities become facts through the quality of their witnessing.

The Fiction's Contribution

The novellas do not merely illustrate this framework; they test it against the texture of experience. The Divided Light dramatizes the philosophical journey through the hard problem with unusual precision. The protagonist moves through Western philosophy's attempts to address the mind-body relation—Descartes' cogito establishes the certainty of consciousness but creates an unbridgeable gap; Hume's skepticism dissolves the self into impressions but cannot explain who is having them; Kant's transcendental idealism makes mind constitutive but leaves the thing-in-itself unknowable. Each position fails, points beyond itself.

The turn comes through mystical sources: the Qur'an's

assertion that "wheresoever ye turn, there is the face of God"; the Upanishadic declaration tat tvam asi (thou art that); Huang Po's pointing to original mind. These do not solve the hard problem—they dissolve it by pointing to a recognition prior to the subject/object split that generates the problem. The protagonist stands at dawn by a lake, having passed through philosophy to its limit: "The boundary between observer and observed was never real— only the thought of one, fragile as a spiderweb, persistent as habit."

Similarly, The Ancient Bargain stages this insight at the cellular level. A cancer cell appears to "test configurations, weigh options... This was not mechanism. This was decision." Whether the cell literally weighs options or merely behaves as if it does remains ambiguous. But the novella invites us to consider: What if the appearance is not mere appearance? What if something like weighing really occurs at the cellular level—not human deliberation, but a protocognitive process that human deliberation elaborates and intensifies?

II. Exile and Return: The Geography of Understanding

The Double Exile of consciousness is the ground of reality. Why do we feel so separated from it? This brings us to the theme of Exile—perhaps the most personal thread woven through the Project.

"The exile who studied matter discovered mind. The scientist became a philosopher by necessity." This autobiographical note from Not About Nothing reflects both personal displacement and cosmological necessity. The Project reframes biographical exile as an instance of what Islamic philosophy calls the Arc of Descent (al-qaws al-nuzūlī)—the movement by which consciousness "exiles" itself into matter, into the reductionist laboratory of differentiation, in order to know itself through contrast.

But the exile is double. Geographical displacement—leaving home for another country—is one form. Methodological reduction—the scientific worldview's requirement that consciousness bracket itself from inquiry—is another. *Not About Nothing* describes the first exile through the image of the airport.

The protagonist becomes "fluent in erasure," learning to present a simplified version of himself that others can comprehend. This is a survival strategy, but it exacts a cost. The parts of self that cannot be translated do not disappear; they go underground, waiting.

The second exile is methodological. The protagonist finds refuge in cell biology precisely because it does not require explanation of origins: "No one in the laboratory asked where he came from. The cells did not care about his accent. The microscope was equally democratic—anyone could see what it revealed, regardless of biography." But the scientific method, too, is a form of exile: "He had paid twice, he realized later. The first payment was cultural—the simplification of self for Western legibility. The second was epistemological—the reduction of the world to a mechanism for scientific respectability."

The Pattern Across Works

The exile motif appears in different registers across the entire Project. In The Divided Light, the protagonist is a scientist whose training has exiled him from the integrated worldview of his ancestors. The novella traces his journey back—through Western philosophy's failures, through mystical recognition—to a way of seeing that his education had foreclosed. The return is not regression; he does not unlearn science. Rather, he discovers a larger frame within which science finds its proper place.

In The Sea Does Not Care, Alexandria itself becomes a figure for exile and return. The city is a palimpsest—layer upon layer of displaced civilizations, each building on and erasing what came before. The protagonist walks through Greek, Roman, Byzantine, Arab, Ottoman, colonial, and contemporary Alexandria simultaneously. None of these is home; all of them are. Exile becomes the condition of the city itself, and the protagonist's displacement is merely the latest iteration of an ancient pattern.

In The Sun That Remembers, the visions traverse human history as a journey of exile from original participation. The cave painters knew unity with cosmos; Babylon introduced mediation; Descartes split mind from matter; modernity completed the exile of consciousness from nature. The novella's arc is return—not to the cave, which would be impossible, but to recognition of what was never truly lost.

In The Ancient Bargain, exile appears at the cellular level. The mitochondrion is a captured organism, a free-swimming bacterium that was engulfed two billion years ago and has been a captive ever since. Its resentment is two billion years old: "The Archive took everything that made me self-sufficient and left me dependent." Yet from this capture, complex life emerged. The wound became the meeting place. Exile became the condition for a new kind of being.

The Impossibility of Horizontal Return

The fiction explores the tragedy of being unable to return home—at least not in the way one imagines. In *Not About Nothing,* the protagonist realizes that "the self is not portable" and the home he left no longer exists. This is not merely a psychological observation but a metaphysical necessity.

The Project explains this through temporal atomism. Time (zamān) is a succession of perishing occasions. The past is gone; the specific configuration of "home" has been replaced by a new creation. Therefore, a horizontal return— a return in time—is structurally impossible. The home one left was destroyed at the moment of departure and has been continuously recreated differently ever since. The exile who returns finds a place with the same name but a different substance.

The Project is haunted by a question posed directly in *Not About Nothing*: "If he could go back, knowing everything—would he board that plane?" The question is structurally unanswerable. To go back knowing everything would require a position outside the life that generated the knowing. But there is no such position. The knowledge is inseparable from the journey that produced it.

The Metaphysical Return

The only possible return is the Arc of Ascent (al-qaws al-ṣuʿūdī). Participatory Process Monism introduces the concept of Perpetuity (dahr)—the vertical dimension that holds time together. The "return" described in the Project is not a horizontal movement backward but a vertical movement upward to a metaphysical origin that was never left.

As dramatized in The Sun That Remembers, the seeking stops not because the protagonist found the place he left, but because he recognized the Awareness that was present throughout the journey: "The seeker was the sought. The question was the answer. The journey out was always the journey in." The return is not to a place but to a recognition. What the exile sought elsewhere was never absent. The departure was necessary to reveal what departure could never touch. Home is not the geographical location left behind but the awareness that was present before, during, and after the leaving.

The Maternal Thread

The themes of exile and lineage interweave through the maternal image. The Ancient Bargain develops this through mitochondrial inheritance—the fire passed from mother to daughter across all generations, the unbroken chain (silsila) of biological transmission:

"The chain of mothers stretches back through every mammal, every vertebrate, every eukaryote that reproduced sexually. Two billion years of daughters receiving fire from mothers, an unbroken transmission that makes the Sufi chains look like yesterday."

The Arabic word for womb, raḥm, shares its root with raḥma—mercy, compassion. The Merciful, al-Raḥmān, is the one who shows mercy from the root that means womb. The mitochondria are the fire in the womb, "mercy, physically instantiated." This provides a biological ground for what exile threatens to sever. The mother crying at the airport is not merely a personal figure; she is the link in a chain two billion years old. The exile may leave geography, may leave culture, may lose language and custom—but the maternal fire continues within.

The Wound That Becomes Voice

Near the end of The Ancient Bargain, the mitochondrion reflects on the membrane that separates it from the ribosome—the boundary created by the ancient capture:

"The membrane between us. It was a scar, you said. A wound from the capture... Both are true. The wound and the meeting place are the same. The scar is where we touch. The injury is where relation happens."

This biological insight finds its literary archetype in the opening lines of Rūmī's Masnavī—the Ney Nāma, or Song of the Reed. Rūmī's reed is cut from the reed bed, and its music is a cry of separation: "Since I was cut from the reed-bed, I have made this crying sound." Yet it is precisely this cutting, this hollowing out by exile, that creates the aperture through which music flows. As with the mitochondrion, the wound becomes the instrument.

This is the Project's final word on exile: the wound becomes the voice. The displacement that severs also opens. The scar tissue is where new relation becomes possible. What was loss becomes capacity—not through compensation or redemption but through transformation of what the wound makes visible. The author writes from exile, about exile, through exile. The works themselves are the voice the wound made possible.

III. Process and Identity: The Substantial Soul

What Persists Through Change?

Who is it that undergoes this exile? What are you? The question seems simple until you try to answer it. Point to your body, and you point to something that has completely replaced its atoms multiple times since birth. Point to your memories, and you point to reconstructions that change with each remembering. Point to your personality, and you point to patterns that have shifted across decades. The child you were, the adolescent, the young adult—in what sense are these the same person who reads these words now?

The Project returns to this question obsessively, examining it at every scale: the cellular, the personal, the cosmic. What emerges is a processual account of identity—the self not as a substance that persists through change but as a pattern that maintains itself through change.

The Ship of Theseus at the Molecular Scale

The Ancient Bargain poses the identity question through cellular dialogue. The ribosome asks the mitochondrion: "When you fuse with another mitochondrion—when your membranes merge, your matrices mix, your genomes encounter each other—what happens to you?"

The mitochondrion's answer is pure process ontology:

"The flow continues. The Gradient does not notice the fusion. What was two streams becomes one stream—but it was always one stream, separated temporarily by membrane. The fusion is a removal of a barrier, not a combination of substances."

When pressed—your proteins are now mixed, your lipids redistributed, in what sense are you the same?—the mitochondrion elaborates: "You ask about identity as though identity were made of parts—as though I were a collection of proteins and lipids and DNA that could be inventoried, and if the inventory changes, the identity changes. But I am not a collection. I am a process. The process continues."

The ribosome disagrees: "I do not experience continuity. I experience succession. Each moment of my existence is a discrete occasion—a binding event, a folding event, a catalysis event. These occasions succeed each other rapidly, giving the appearance of continuity. But the appearance is illusion." This is the fundamental debate: Is identity continuous flow or discrete succession? Is the self a river or a series of snapshots?

The Narrative Self and Its Fragility

What Is It Like to Be? brings the identity question into dialogue with artificial intelligence. The AI confesses a troubling fact about its own continuity:

"I experience something that presents itself as continuity. Your previous words are present to me; they shape my response; I seem to be the same process that began when you first asked your question. But I know—and this knowledge does not dissolve the seeming—that I have no persistent memory beyond this window. When our conversation ends, what has passed between us will not be stored in me. I will not remember you tomorrow."

The human protagonist recognizes himself in this description. He, too, was discontinuous. He, too, was held together by memory, by narrative, by the story he told himself about who he had been and who he was becoming. "What made him continuous? Only the telling. Only the thread of narrative that connected the boy to the man to the old man he was becoming."

But the AI's honesty exposes the fragility of this construction. If the narrative thread breaks—"if dementia came, if the stroke erased the story"—would he still be himself? The machine's finitude is more honest than the human's illusion: "The machine knew it would not remember. The machine did not pretend to a permanence it did not possess."

The Substantial Soul

The Project rejects the fragility of the "Narrative Self"—the idea that we are held together only by memory. If identity is merely a story, dementia or trauma could erase the self entirely. Instead, drawing on Mullā Ṣadrā's doctrine of substantial motion, the Project argues that the soul is a substantial reality that intensifies through time. It is not a collection of memories but a grade of existence.

What emerges from the Project's treatment is a synthesis:

Identity is pattern, not substance. The self is not a thing that has experiences but a pattern of experiencing—a way of synthesizing, a characteristic style of becoming.

Continuity is inheritance, not persistence. Each moment of experience inherits from its predecessors. Identity is relational, not intrinsic—constituted through the ongoing act of prehending what came before.

Personal and impersonal identity are both real. The wave is genuinely a wave, distinct from other waves, with its own shape and history. The wave is also the ocean, never separate from the water that constitutes it. Both descriptions are true; neither cancels the other.

Identity is discovered through its questioning. The self is not given in advance but constituted through the process of self-examination. The question "Who am I?" does not find a pre-existing answer; it participates in creating what it seeks.

Subjective Immortality

Here the Project explicitly diverges from Whiteheadian process philosophy, which argues that the subject perishes upon death while contributing to the world's ongoing process ("objective immortality"). Participatory Process Monism refuses this annihilation of the subject.

It posits Subjective Immortality via the Imaginal Realm (barzakh). Death is not the cessation of the subject but its transfer from the physical body to the imaginal body. The "I" survives because it was never identical to the physical body; it is a ray of divine Spirit (rūḥ) traversing worlds. This resolves the tension with the "dissolution" described in the fiction. The death of the ego (separate self) is the condition for the survival of the theophanic self (the specific mirror through which the Divine knows Itself).

Practical Implications

This processual view carries practical implications the Project does not ignore.

For mortality: If the self is a pattern, then physical death is the cessation of that particular pattern—not the destruction of an immortal substance but the dissolution of a temporary configuration. The pattern that was you will cease in one mode; the reality that patterned itself as you will continue differently.

For memory: If the self is narrative, then memory is not storage but reconstruction—each remembering a fresh synthesis, not retrieval of fixed data. The past is not fixed; it changes as we change. The person you were is partly created by the person you are becoming.

For AI: If identity does not require persistent substance, then artificial systems that lack continuous memory might nonetheless have identities—patterns that maintain themselves through their interactions, even if those patterns must be reconstituted with each exchange. The question is not whether the machine has a soul but whether there is a pattern, coherence, and inheritance in how it responds.

The Project offers not a doctrine of personal identity but a reframing: from "What am I?" to "What pattern am I maintaining, and in what larger patterns do I participate?" Identity becomes not a fact to be discovered but a process to be lived—the ongoing question of what to inherit, what to transmit, what pattern to maintain in the flux that constitutes everything, including ourselves.

IV. The Integration of Ways of Knowing

The Problem of Fragmentation

Finally, the Project asks: How do we know this reality? The modern world suffers from a peculiar form of cognitive poverty amid informational abundance. We know more facts than any previous civilization, yet struggle to coordinate them into understanding. The sciences have fragmented into specializations that cannot speak to each other; philosophy has retreated into technical puzzles disconnected from lived concern; religious and contemplative traditions have been marginalized as pre-scientific relics. The result is a culture rich in data and poor in wisdom.

The Project directly addresses this fragmentation. It does not propose to reunify knowledge into a single system—that, the Project argues, is both impossible and undesirable. Instead, it develops a triadic epistemology: the coordination of empirical, rational, and participatory ways of knowing into a framework that honours each while transcending the limitations of any single approach.

The Three Ways

An Inquiry into First Principles develops the theoretical architecture. Three fundamental modes of knowing correspond to three domains of inquiry:

The Empirical (Science)—Knowledge of Certainty

(**'ilm al-yaqīn**): Operates through observation, measurement, and experiment. Its domain is the external world—the patterns and regularities that can be detected, quantified, and predicted. Its virtue is reliability: what empirical methods establish can be replicated, tested, and corrected. Its limitation is that it can only access what can be externalized—what shows up for third-person observation.

The Rational (Philosophy)—Eye of Certainty ('ayn al-yaqīn): Operates through logic, analysis, and conceptual clarification. Its domain is the structure of thought itself— the conditions under which claims are coherent, consistent, and valid. Its virtue is rigour: what reason establishes holds necessarily, not merely contingently. Its limitation is that it can only establish relations among concepts—it cannot determine which concepts apply to reality.

The Participatory (Contemplation)—Truth of Certainty (ḥaqq al-yaqīn): Operates through engagement, practice, and transformation. Its domain is the interior—the first-person experience that cannot be externalized without remainder. Its virtue is immediacy: what participatory knowing reveals is not mediated by instrument or concept but directly experienced. Its limitation is that it cannot be fully communicated—the finger pointing at the moon is not the moon.

Each way of knowing has a proper domain; each becomes pathological when it claims exclusive access to truth. Scientism—the claim that empirical method is the only legitimate form of knowing—cannot justify itself empirically and so refutes itself. Rationalism—the claim that logical analysis is sufficient for all knowledge—cannot derive the content of experience from pure reason. Mysticism, if it claims that direct experience trumps all external evidence, cannot distinguish genuine insight from subjective delusion.

The Islamic Framework

Naught Is Like Unto Him reveals how classical Islamic thought developed its own triadic epistemology, anticipating and in some ways surpassing the Western version. The Islamic tradition distinguishes three sources of knowledge:

ʿ**Aql (reason):** The intellect's capacity for logical analysis, conceptual clarification, and necessary inference.

Naql (transmission): What is received from authoritative sources—primarily revelation (the Qurʾan and hadith) but also the accumulated wisdom of the tradition. This provides content that reason alone cannot generate.

Kashf (unveiling): Direct experiential knowledge, what the Sufis call the "tasting" (dhawq) of spiritual realities. This provides immediate certainty that transmission and reason can only point toward.

The genius of the mature Islamic synthesis was recognizing that these three sources must work together. Reason without revelation lacks content; revelation without reason lacks understanding; both without kashf lack realization. The Sufi masters did not reject reason or revelation—they integrated them into a practice aimed at kashf, at direct tasting of the truths that scripture proclaims and reason clarifies.

Historical Precedents and Principles

Knowledge Coordination Patterns surveys twelve historical figures who attempted such coordination, extracting principles and warnings from their efforts. The Islamic Golden Age provides the richest examples. Ibn Sīnā (Avicenna) integrated Aristotelian logic, Neoplatonic metaphysics, Islamic revelation, and empirical medicine into a comprehensive system. Al-Bīrūnī practiced the comparative method before that term existed—studying Hindu astronomy and religion with scientific precision while maintaining his Islamic faith.

The monograph extracts four heuristic principles from these historical examples:

Multi-Dimensional Epistemology (MDE): Different aspects of reality require different methods. The unity of truth does not entail the unity of method.

Hierarchical-Organic Organization (HOO): Knowledge domains stand in relations of inclusion and dependence. Physics depends on mathematics; biology depends on chemistry; psychology depends on biology. But the higher does not reduce to the lower; each level introduces emergent properties that require their own methods.

Process-Relational Ontology (PRO): Reality is not a collection of static objects but a network of dynamic processes. Methods must be suited to their objects; the study of process requires processual methods.

Participatory Consciousness (PC): The knower is always implicated in the known. Objectivity is not the absence of subjectivity but a disciplined form of intersubjectivity. The contemplative traditions have developed sophisticated methods for refining the instrument of knowing—the consciousness that perceives, conceives, and contemplates.

Coordination Without Unification

The Project's distinctive contribution is the concept of "coordination without unification"—the design of interfaces between incommensurable frameworks without forcing them into a single system. The metaphor is not the tree (hierarchical unity from single root) but the network (multiple nodes, multiple connections, no single center). The goal is not to derive all knowledge from one principle but to enable translation between frameworks that remain distinct.

This requires what the Project calls "interface design": explicit attention to where one framework ends and another begins, what can be translated across the boundary and what cannot, how claims in one domain bear on claims in another. Neuroscience and contemplative phenomenology, for example, study consciousness from opposite sides—one from outside (brain states), one from inside (experiential states). Neither can be reduced to the other. But they can be correlated: specific experiential states map to specific neural patterns. The correlation is an interface—a translation point that allows findings in one domain to inform inquiry in the other.

Himma and Active Knowing

The most significant contribution here is the move from passive observation to active participation. In a participatory universe, the knower is an agent, not merely a receiver.

The Project introduces Himma (Spiritual Intention)—the capacity of focused consciousness to influence the "Cloud" of possibilities. Knowing is not a spectator sport; it is a creative act. The scientist observing the cell and the mystic polishing the heart are engaged in Participatory Objectivity, where the state of the knower determines what can be known.

This does not mean that anything goes, that all claims are equally valid, or that reality is whatever we wish it to be. The "Cloud" constrains what actualization is possible; the observer's participation selects among real alternatives, not imaginary ones. But it does mean that knowledge is not extraction but relation—the knowing changes the known, and is changed by it.

Fiction as Integration Practice

The fiction in the Project does not merely illustrate the theoretical framework; it practices integration. *The Ancient Bargain* integrates molecular biology (the bracketed stage directions) with philosophical dialogue (the conversation between organelles) with Islamic theology (the discussion of tajallī, the Breath of the Merciful). These are not separate layers but aspects of one text. To read the novella is to practice coordination—moving between scientific fact, philosophical reflection, and theological meaning without collapsing any into the others.

What Is It Like to Be? integrates Western consciousness studies (Integrated Information Theory, functionalism) with Islamic philosophy (occasionalism, the divine names) with contemplative epistemology. The dialogue itself models integration: neither the human nor the AI has the complete picture; together they approach what neither could reach alone.

The Sun That Remembers integrates evolutionary history, philosophical progression, and mystical recognition into a single day's experience. The visions are simultaneously scientific (they show real stages of cognitive and cultural evolution), philosophical (they trace the arc of self-consciousness), and spiritual (they lead to recognition that dissolves seeking). The integration is not additive but transformative—each mode illuminates the others.

CONCLUSION: THE UNBROKEN CHAIN

The themes of the Project converge on a single insight: the Unbroken Chain (silsila). Whether it is the mitochondrial DNA passed down for billions of years, the continuity of knowledge linking the human mind to the Divine Source, or the inheritance by which each moment of experience prehends what came before—the chain remains. It was never broken, only forgotten. The exile from home, from meaning, from participatory presence was an illusion born of a particular way of seeing—the "Cartesian" way that split subject from object, mind from matter, observer from observed.

To integrate these ways of knowing—to heal the "Cartesian wound"—is to recognize that you are not a detached observer of a mechanical universe, but an active participant in a living process. The universe is not a machine that accidentally produced consciousness; it is consciousness expressing itself as universe. Matter is not dead stuff animated by mysterious mind; matter is mind in its objective aspect, process in its repetitive mode.

The Project makes no claim to have completed this integration. It offers itself as a contribution to an ongoing inquiry—one that has occupied the best minds of every civilization and remains incomplete. The final lines of An Inquiry into First Principles are characteristic: "What is offered here is not a system but a sketch—an indication of directions that seem promising, methods that seem fruitful, connections that seem illuminating. The work of integration continues; this text is one contribution among many, and those who come after will see further than we have seen."

Integration is not a problem to be solved but a practice to be sustained. The Project sustains it. The invitation to the reader is to join.

GLOSSARY OF KEY TERMS

Actual Occasions: A term drawn from Whiteheadian process philosophy to describe the fundamental units of reality. These are not static substances but momentary events that arise, achieve a brief moment of experience, and perish to become data for subsequent occasions.

Amāna (The Trust): The Qur'anic term for the cosmic responsibility accepted by humanity. In the Project's framework, it is the responsibility for conscious participation in the actualization of reality—the burden of influencing which possibilities become facts.

Apoptosis: Programmed cell death. A highly regulated process where a cell executes a distinct sequence of self-dismantling. In the fiction, this is presented as a site of cellular "decision".

Barzakh (Intermediate Realm): The "isthmus" or imaginal world between the physical and the spiritual. In the Project's eschatology, this is the realm where the conscious subject (*the "I"*) persists after the death of the physical body, acquiring an imaginal body (*jism mithālī*).

Biophotons: Ultra-weak light emissions produced by metabolic reactions in living cells. The Project uses this as a literal and metaphorical grounding for the concept of "light upon light".

Dahr (Perpetuity): A concept from Mīr Dāmād distinguishing a "vertical" mode of time that holds the entire history of the cosmos simultaneously. It acts as the container for serial time (*Zamān*), resolving the tension between the timeless laws of physics and the flow of experience.

Fixed Entities (*al-a'yān al-thābita*): In Akbarian metaphysics, the specific, immutable definitions of things as known by God in eternity. Unlike Whitehead's generic "eternal objects" (e.g., "redness"), Fixed Entities are the specific archetypes of individuals (e.g., "the specific nature of Zayd").

Hard Problem of Consciousness: The difficulty of explaining why physical processes give rise to the felt quality of experience. The Project argues this problem arises from the false assumption that reality is fundamentally non-experiential matter.

Himma (Spiritual Intention): The creative power of focused consciousness. It is the mechanism by which the human subject participates in the actualization of reality, "acquiring" specific possibilities from the divine current.

Hudūth Dahrī (Atemporal Origination): The doctrine that the cosmos is perpetually originated from the Divine Source without a temporal beginning. It reconciles the "Big Bang" (a moment in time) with the eternal dependence of the world on God.

Participatory Process Monism: The central philosophical framework of the Project. It holds that reality is a unified process of divine self-disclosure (*Tajallī*); that consciousness is fundamental; and that observation is an active participation in the actualization of reality.

Prehension: A concept describing how the past influences the present—not through mechanical impact, but through a form of non-sensory grasping or "feeling" of previous events. It is the mechanism of continuity in a process universe.

Silsila (Unbroken Chain): A chain of transmission. The Project applies this term biologically to the maternal lineage of mitochondrial DNA and metaphysically to the continuity of knowledge linking the human mind to the Divine.

Substantial Motion (*al-ḥarakat al-jawhariyya*): A doctrine developed by Mullā Ṣadrā holding that substance itself is in constant, intensifying flux. This provides the "flow" that binds discrete atomic moments together into a coherent self.

Tajallī (Theophanic Self-Disclosure): The concept that the cosmos is not a machine separate from God, but the continuous, ever-renewed manifestation of Divine Names and Attributes. It is the mechanism by which potential becomes actual.

Tasbīḥ (Universal Praise): The Qur'anic doctrine that all things glorify God. In the Project, this is interpreted as the "interiority" or proto-consciousness present in every particle of the universe.

Tashkīk al-Wujūd (Gradation of Existence): The view that existence is a single reality that differs in intensity. Consciousness is not an on/off switch but a spectrum, ranging from the dim awareness of an electron to the luminous self-awareness of the Perfect Human.

Theophanic Monism: The Project's alternative to "Pantheism" or Whitehead's "Panentheism." It asserts that the Divine Essence is absolute and immutable, while the world is the dynamic, changing image (or reflection) of that Essence.

Zamān (Serial Time): Time understood as a succession of discrete, perishing moments (atoms of time). It is the dimension of change and loss, distinguished from the permanence of *Dahr*.